Pook's Curiosity Shop

So many readers requested a sequel to *Pook in Business* that *Pook's Curiosity Shop* was a must.

This time Pook enters the high class antique world in partnership with the beautiful Olga, and financed by Honners. At once we plunge into the antique dealer's life of auctions, private buying and other means of unearthing the treasures essential to this unique trade.

Set against Pook's accurate background of business practice we see our hero encounter the hazards of the profession in the shape of eccentric dealers, awkward customers and difficult situations. In his search for success Pook meets the girl of his dreams, the lovely female Viking called Tora, while Olga is wooed by Yosseff, a wealthy Arab prince.

The resultant havoc is a hilarious romance, but the book will have an additional appeal to everybody who has paused by the window of an old curiosity shop.

By the same author:

Peter Pook

Pook's Curiosity Shop

ROBERT HALE · LONDON

© Peter Pook 1977
First published in Great Britain 1977

ISBN 0 7091 6122 0

Robert Hale Limited
Clerkenwell House
Clerkenwell Green
London EC1R 0HT

Printed in Great Britain by
Clarke, Doble & Brendon Ltd,
Plymouth and London

To my adoring wife, Val Manning, for dedicating *her* latest novel to me.

1

When a big operator like me goes into business he needs premises in the heart of the city among the commercial giants along High Street. With my kind of capital there is only one way to do this. You select a site between Tesco and Boots, then during each evening you wheel your hot chestnuts barrow there and park it to catch the cinema trade.

But you can't conduct an antiques' gallery from a barrow, so you find a shop as near High Street as possible without having to visit Tesco by bus. I found Mortimer's Hairdressing Salon midway down London Road—a business thoroughfare aptly named because it led to London when one left Cudford, and as Mortimer's was number 975 I gained the impression that it was nearer London than Cudford. London Road actually started from High Street—'Adjacent Main Multiple Shopping Area' the advert stated, but what it did not state was that London Road was one of the longest streets in Britain, like a motorway with shops, and to reach number 975 I walked as far as I could, then boarded a bus.

Another interesting point about Mortimer's was the ancient red-tiled roof and walls above the shop. I discovered later that these dated back to 1700, when the building had been a farmhouse in the village of Half Horseball Norton on the turnpike road to London, before being swallowed up by Cudford.

The shop was vacant because Mr Mortimer had died at an advanced age, though rumour had it that he had drowned. Drowned very slowly over a period of some sixty years in the public bar of the Flying Bull Inn, an ordeal which had given him a nose similar to a mandarin orange. Hence I was able to purchase the premises freehold for what would appear to be a ridiculous price today of £2,100—'inc. goodwill, fix. & fittings'.

Both goodwill and fixtures were to give me considerable problems in the months ahead when I was struggling to convert the premises from a barber-shop to an antique gallery. Although I had painted over the facia-board my new trade name of *Nostalgia*, customers still entered demanding a short-back-and-sides, shampoo and singe. Another aspect of the goodwill took the form of customers who insisted they should escort me next door to the Flying Bull for a hair tonic, as they phrased it. Some of them who had already visited the Flying Bull called me Harold and inquired how my gout was, or asked if my old woman was still at it.

The fittings and fixtures were a big stumbling block, being in the main irremovable. The five great shampoo basins might have come from Ancient Rome, let into solid blocks of white marble which apparently held up that side of the building. I feared that any attempt to remove them would lead to the collapse of the party wall I shared with the butcher next door. The walls themselves were decorated with massive Edwardian plate-glass mirrors inscribed with gold Gothic lettering exhorting us to use Parker's Pomade in our fight against dandruff, baldness and grey hair. I proved by experiment that these mirrors were also irremovable, being welded to the walls by huge plugs, as though the craftsmen of the Edwardian

8

era feared that one day Cudford would be the centre of an earthquake zone and consequently we must needs trade from retail forts.

Another prominent snag was the barber's pole outside the shop on the right hand side, painted in the traditional red-and-white spiral to inform the passing carriage folk that here they could have their wigs combed and powdered. This nine-foot pole left me weak and trembling in my efforts to remove it. The securing bolts had long since rusted into the clamps, making me feel I was struggling to remove the bowsprit from HMS *Victory* single-handed. Nor could I saw it into sections, for time and weather seemed to have fossilized the wood into a kind of bog-oak. Eventually I solved the problem by affixing a metal plate to the pole which bore the legend: 'Rare example of Medieval Maypole, *circa* A.D. 1400, originally set up at Half Horseball Norton's annual Maid-and-Shepherds Fair, 1297–1836.'

Oddly enough, this exhibit was to become such a success that I could have sold it time and again to the American market if only I could have wrenched it from the building. However, necessity being the mother of invention, I arranged for our local carpenter, Gus Piper, to supply me with medieval maypoles which he constructed from as many old boat masts as I could lay hands on.

As you may remember from *Pook in Business*, I had served a hard apprenticeship to the trade of some nine years, starting off without knowing a thing about it, yet staving off bankruptcy until my premises had become so valuable because of regional development that I was able to make a profit at last by selling the shop itself.

This time Olga was determined I should make good, so she

began reforming me right from the start. I don't know if you have ever experienced women trouble, and I don't know if you have ever suffered business problems, but if you've ever had them both together you have my sympathy. Olga's current campaign was to stop me smoking so we could meet the mortgage payments and keep me fitter for work. I assured her that smoking was the only vice left to me; that without it I should be unbearable. She thought this was strange because I was unbearable with it. I assured her that it was perfectly normal in our English climate to have a cough from November to May—in fact, foreigners dubbed it the English malaise. I showed her how smoking did actually stop coughing if she would let me have a cigarette—as it did for a full ten minutes.

But Olga was adamant that I give it up completely. To this end she took me to church with a mouth full of boiled sweets in order to strengthen my resolve and to put the Arch-bishop of Canterbury between me and tobacco. In my pocket reposed a packet of twenty, supplied by Olga so that I should never feel completely cut off from the habit. Unfortunately I had smoked them the moment her back was turned.

"No need to worry any more, Peter," Olga informed me as we sang *Fight the Good Fight*. "Always remember there's the sealed packet of twenty in your pocket to boost your morale, and the boiled sweets will take away the craving."

I smiled gratefully at Olga over the hymn-book, thinking how handy the altar candles would be to light up from. I felt guilty as only a smoker can, standing there with the empty packet in my pocket, a half empty packet hidden in my waistband, a box of matches secreted in a handkerchief and six panatella cigars lodged in the top of my right sock. Also about my person was a tiny box of snuff and a deodorant aerosol for my mouth.

"Thank you for helping me give it up, love," I mumbled, wondering if her sensitive nostrils would smell the tobacco warehouse standing next to her. My sense of guilt was so strong in this religious environment that I momentarily feared I might be punished by bursting into flames, like the burning bush.

"Smell the incense, Peter—that's all the smoke you should ever inhale," Olga smiled, sucking her share of it through her lovely nostrils.

I had already noted the censer with interest, a figured brass objet d'art circa Late Georgian that would look well in my shop. Throughout the hymn and the Lesson about driving the money-changers from the Temple it dawned on me more and more how this beautiful old church resembled a high-class Antiques' Gallery with music. The bronze Lectern and the silver candlesticks particularly caught my eye, so I made a mental note to call on the Vicar as soon as possible.

Where I had gone wrong on my last venture in this field was my inability to resist the junk side of the business. Most of the junk came with the good pieces, especially at auction sales, so that one prize of a Victorian brass lantern clock with a French movement would be knocked down to you with its accompanying retinue of fairground china, bamboo pot-stand, Edwardian multi-knife-polisher, trousers-press and twelve rolls of wallpaper. Junk came in even larger quantities when you cleared a house, right from the perks in the parlour to the mops in the scullery.

Junk sells fast but unfortunately it ruins the classy side of the business, like selling crashed car components in a Rolls showroom. So I had brought Olga into the business to keep it strictly haut monde, uncluttered by the push-chairs, jelly moulds and assorted magazines of the general dealer. She was an excellent salesgirl, having long replaced the dog as man's best friend, and, wearing her little black dress, as she always phrased it, could certainly handle the male clients.

"Peter, meet Yosseff," she said, soon after we had opened. "Yosseff is studying over here. He is a prince."

Yosseff held up his beringed hands. "Not a prince, my pretty one, please. In my country I am nothing, just a mere princeling. But for our oil I should be poor."

"Does he intend buying anything?" I whispered urgently, taken aback by this handsome student with the white teeth.

"Wants to buy me!" Olga hissed with wide eyes.

"What did he offer?"

"He's rich. Will buy the shop plus stock if I go with it."

"How rich?"

"Well, I don't know what sort of a grant he gets for college, but his private income is £1,327,480 per annum, tax free. It's the oil, you know."

"Is he at Cudford University, Olga?"

"Yes, darling. Says he is learning so much there about geology that he would like to buy the place at the end of the course and take it back home with him. Isn't he ridiculously dishy, Peter, even in European clothes!"

"And no camel."

"Don't be jealous, Peter, just because he says I'm the most ravishing creature he has ever met."

"Pretty quiet in the desert, dear. Maybe you're the first woman he's seen."

"Oh, he's so incredibly romantic and dreamy—I could give myself to him over the counter."

"Move the glass and china clear first, Olga."

I did not worry over much because Olga could always handle the fellows, and she certainly attracted business. Sometimes she seemed to think I was not the world's greatest lover, but as I told her, the highest romance of all was the thrill of commerce. With feminine meticulousness Olga was stocking only good class merchandise, which she catalogued and ticketed as if we were Bond Street. The trash she threw out ruthlessly, often directly into my lap if small enough, or into the yard when I carted home double-beds and picture-frames.

"Price your space, Peter, and stop crying over the junk," she counselled me. "You have to choose between a thirty bob pram and an Edwardian inlaid mahogany china cabinet at sixty guineas."

"But the pram cost us nothing, Olga. They threw it in so I could carry away all these potted plants, free."

"Those plants died soon after you were born. Now you've got eight sticks of fossilized wood embedded in concrete."

"We can still sell the pots, Olga—tanner a time."

Olga sighed. "Why don't you go the whole hog and set up as a rag-and-bone man with a barrow? We could fill the windows with scrap-iron and jam jars."

"You're so right, Olga."

She was right, of course, but the waste appalled me. I took all the junk I could manage round to my general dealer friends, like Eddie Flaxmon who sold everything from a bath with geyser still attached to it, down to old copies of *John Bull* magazine. They did not pay me a fortune but at least it kept me in petrol for my station-wagon. This vehicle was surmounted by a huge roof-rack, seven feet long by four feet wide, that would carry anything up to a three-piece suite—

the two armchairs cradled in the settee. Behind I towed my trailer, converted from a horse-box, so I had virtually a one-man pantechnicon. This ensured us cheap speedy transport available at all times, so essential in this business.

Olga transformed the showroom, as she now called our shop, by having me decorate the place with three coats of emulsion paint. Her colour scheme consisted of Egyptian Gold Walls, white woodwork and wine red drapes—real classy effect when completed. I solved the problem of the marble basins by boarding them over to form a long display counter down one side of the showroom.

The worst expense was the deep wine carpet, wall to wall, upon which began to appear familiar objets d'art ticketed with very unfamiliar names. In fact I had never heard of them. For instance, a Victorian ebonized sideboard with glazed ends was now listed as a Period Credenza, and an Edwardian inlaid mahogany china cabinet turned out to be a Superb Vitrine. An Edwardian inlaid rosewood writing-table with inset leather top proved to be a Lady's Bonheur du Jour.

"How on earth were you in the trade so long, yet learned so little, Peter?" Olga demanded, hearing my exclamations of "Fancy that!" and "You could have fooled me!" as I walked round the exhibits.

"That is a trade secret, darling," I jested.

"I'll tell you why. Because you suffered from junk on the brain, that's why. You were so engrossed in selling sixpenny gas-brackets and flock mattresses that you went bust."

"And I didn't have your exquisite taste, Olga. I bought all wrong, then chased the pennies instead of the pounds. I was my own worst enemy. The miracle was I lasted so long. I should be thankful I've got you behind me now—as you

know I am." Agreeing wholeheartedly with Olga on everything not only saved time and energy but also took her mind
off one's shortcomings. Otherwise she was liable to drag up
smoking when she wasn't with me to act as chaperon between
myself and the Devil. Personally, I found it pretty tough
being a man and having to cope with tobacco, drink, horses
and women, none of which bothered Olga at all.

"How do you like the decor of the showroom, now, Peter?"

"Just can't recognize the place, dear. A fantastic job.
Flowers too. Let's only hope we can sell the stuff and pay
Honners his interest."

My old friends Honners—the Hon. Lesley Pilkington-
Goldberg—had put up all the cash for our venture, and he
called every day to ensure that his money was safe or at
least being properly used.

"You have to speculate before you can accumulate, Peter.
Don't expect a fortune overnight."

"The awful thing about establishing a business is the out-
lay, dear. Nothing coming in, yet money pouring out in
every direction. At least when I was broke there was practically no expenditure."

Olga smiled her beautiful smile which was to become
familiar to me as her successful sales smile. "The tide has
turned already, Peter. I have made our first sale. Remember
Item 7, late Victorian Samovar in Burnished Copper which I
purchased for £10? Well, I have sold same for twenty-five
guineas!"

"Collapse of stout partner! Brilliant! Who bought it,
dear?"

"Yosseff. He has decided to collect special pieces to take
back to his palace when he finally leaves Britain."

"Good work, honey, but isn't that an awful lot of profit?"

"In our business one charges what the market will pay. I went to great trouble buying that samovar, and you spent nearly half a day polishing it up from black with Brillo pads, so our profit is not excessive. You go out and buy the right goods at the right prices, then leave me to sell them to our best advantage."

I looked at Olga with new admiration. We were trading in the happy days before Value Added Tax, and before those excellent television programmes had popularized antiques to the extent that nothing was sacred any more, prices rocketed and bargains became almost non-existent. The days when dealers were still breaking up Victorian washstands as useless and throwing out brass bedsteads for scrap. But best of all they were the days when exciting finds could be made for next to nothing, even at the auction sales. By today's standards we bought ridiculously cheap and sold ridiculously cheap, but there was a worthwhile profit in between. In my previous business I grossed three pounds for every pound I spent, but as the job was labour-intensive I certainly earned it—bargaining, transporting, repairing, cleaning and polishing.

Just to make your mouth water—and a dealer's heart bleed—we were buying walnut canterburys and dumb-waiters for thirty shillings, mahogany knee-hole desks for seven pounds, tub chairs for two pounds, brass fire-irons for a pound or less, and rosewood sideboards for three pounds. On the other hand, you could still rent a shop for two pounds a week and if you could net a thousand a year you felt like a millionaire.

"Now, Peter, your job is to supply me with stock—I'll do

the vending," Olga told me at our Daily Orders meeting. "Don't waste time in the Bold Forester because those lay-abouts in there are a bad influence on you."

"Birds of a feather flock together, Olga," I agreed.

"Go straight to Mellon's Auction Galleries and bid for the items I have marked, but don't get carried away and pay more than I have pencilled in, understand?"

"A fool and his money are soon parted, Olga."

"Mind you're early so you can get a good position right underneath Mr Mellon's nose on the rostrum."

"The early bird catches the worm, Olga."

"And the late bird catches the woodworm, Peter, and we don't want any of that—it's the trade's worst nightmare. The porters know about that, so ask their advice but remember to tip them."

"A bob a nod is the rate for the job, Olga."

"Yes, and if something is going ridiculously cheap catch the porter's eye and perhaps have a little flutter."

"Cast your bread upon the waters, Olga."

"Don't gossip to the other dealers, Peter; concentrate on the bidding every second—even if you're not in it just then."

"He who hesitates is lost, Olga."

"But have inexhaustible patience, then come in with your bid bang on the psychological moment."

"Rome wasn't built in a day, Olga—strike while the iron is hot."

"Now, if the bidding is too keen force yourself to withdraw."

"He who bids and runs away lives to bid another day. If in doubt drop out, Olga."

"And don't make your old mistake of arguing with Mr

Mellon if he beats you to it with his hammer."

"Never complain, never explain, Olga."

"So keep your temper and be polite to Mr Mellon at all times."

"A civil tongue costs nothing, Olga."

"But when you do land a prize don't go boasting to the other dealers around you, Peter."

"An empty kettle makes most noise, Olga. A still tongue in a wise head. Don't make other people as wise as yourself, Olga."

Olga regarded me quizzically. "Peter, you sound more like a parrot every day. In fact you're beginning to look like one."

"Who's a pretty boy now then?" I squawked. Olga counselled me thus daily, and experience had taught me that it paid to reply with the wisdom of the ages because that is the one thing difficult for anybody to contradict.

"Finally, Peter, don't you dare smoke while you're out of my sight, understand? I shall know it if you do."

"Smoke in that dangerous place, Olga! That's how the Great Fire of London started. Why, it would be like striking a match in a coalmine. So there's No Smoking signs round the walls."

"I am well aware how those other dealers smoke on the quiet behind piles of furniture, Peter. That Wally Tate is the worst offender—I saw him puffing away inside a huge Edwardian wardrobe once."

"Mr Mellon even has a No Smoking sign pinned to his rostrum."

"Solely to stop those blessed dealers setting fire to him as they bid, Peter. As it is it's a wonder he can see through the fug to take bids from the rear of the hall. I can't understand it; smoking strictly prohibited yet the place is blue up to the ceiling. Mark my words, one day that lot will go up like a torch and everybody will be trapped inside."

"Always use a long spoon when you sup with the Devil, Olga."

"I can't help feeling, Peter, that lately your conversation has lost some of its sparkle. Sometimes I wonder if I am speaking to some kind of calendar with a tear-off motto for each day."

"Never judge a sausage by its skin, dear."

"So you're a talking sausage after all. Still, I expect giving up cigarettes is a strain on your nerves, eh?"

"If nerves can have hernia that's what they've got, Olga. My head feels as if it may implode at any moment, like a busted television tube. Then I get dizzy spells followed by hot flushes and nausea."

"So in actual fact you're pregnant. For goodness sake be a man and face up to life, Peter."

"I could face up to it much beter if I could have a fag, Olga. Doctors recommend the gradual withdrawal method to prevent addicts like me going potty. Wally Tate is on it and now he's cut right down to forty a day. Only he can't use matches any more because he shakes them all over the shop when he opens the box."

"But you're not a weakling like Wally Tate, Peter."

"I'm taller than he is too."

"I mean will power, Peter. You're a man of iron resolution, as you've told me so often. You laugh at temptation."

"Ha-ha-ha-ha! Now can I have a fag, Olga? Just one to strengthen my will power—please?"

"Peter—stop that nonsense! Where are your boiled sweets?"

"One more boiled sweet and I shall throw up, Olga. They're hinting in the Bold Forester that my presence turns the beer off."

"Then don't go in there, as I told you before. Now hurry along to the sale-room and concentrate on the day's business."

Leaving Olga to polish a Late Victorian mahogany shaving stand with boxwood inlay and shield mirror, I fled to the car. Safely round the block I lit up skilfully with one hand, then drove to the Mellon Auction Galleries better prepared for the battle of the bids against my fellow bandits.

2

Forty years on the public rostrum had made Mr Mellon rather cynical about the human race, especially the species *Dealerius Greedibus* as he called us. He divided us into three sub-species known as First Class Bandits who sought the plums, Second Class Bandits who purchased the bulk of his wares, and Third Class Bandits—also referred to as Dustbins—who took the rubbish.

Formerly I had been a Dustbin, but now Olga was behind me I had been promoted to a Second Class Bandit. Right at the summit of the First Class Bandits stood the Ring—a select cartel of dealers who combined to prevent their bidding against each other for the cream of the catalogue.

Long ago the Mellon Auction Galleries had been a cinema, but now the large building was packed with goods of every description which Mr Mellon auctioned off three days a week, like a great general of yore commanding his troops on a battle-field of furniture. Looking not unlike Sir Winston Churchill, Mr Mellon removed his reading glasses with a flourish to harangue the assembled army drawn up on all sides round his rostrum.

"Those of you who have known me for nigh on half a century," Mr Mellon boomed, waving his spectacles on high to denote the passage of time, "will be aware that I do not conduct this sale for any charitable institution—such as a

21

Home for Aged Dealers. Nor is it my function to distribute
free furniture to the deserving poor. Therefore may I be so
bold as to implore you to make realistic bids for the lots,
because, ladies and gentlemen, even in this age of monetary
crisis and industrial depression you cannot fairly expect to
purchase a handsome winged three-piece suite in uncut
moquette for five shillings."

Mr Mellon's rhetoric was caused by Wally Tate, whose
opening bid—even when the auctioneer had invited a nominal
starter of ten pounds—was invariably the same, delivered in
a tone of utter dejection: "Take a dollar, Guvner!" This
opening gambit so condemned the lot as valueless in the eyes
of the general public that often it would be the sole offer,
followed by a stunned silence all round.

"Take a dollar, Guvner," Walley droned, breaking the
silence, completely impervious to rhetoric.

Wally's wan expressionless face below his cloth cap was
punctuated in the centre by a glowing cigarette butt that
never seemed to go out, as though he wore it there per-
manently like other men wear glasses or hearing aids. He
possessed that rare gift of being able to infuriate Mr Mellon
merely by standing motionless.

"I shall ignore the kiss of death from our local Dick Turpin
and appeal to the normal human beings present for a reasonable bid," Mr Mellon barked. "Will somebody kindly start
me at ten pounds?"

"Take a dollar, Guvner."

"Shut up, man! Begging and soliciting for alms are strictly
prohibited on these premises. Now, do I hear a bid of eight
pounds perhaps for this magnificent three-piece? Or do you
wish me to withdraw it from the sale?"

22

"One pound!"

Everybody looked round to locate the fresh voice and I discovered they were all staring at me. The realization hit me that I had involuntarily shouted out the one pound offer and I knew Olga would kill me if she was present. I waited with sweating lack of confidence for the next bid to clear me. Now I had broken the ice the other dealers would pounce; even the Gentiles—as we called the general public who patronized auctions instead of buying from us—would be drawn in. But there was that morbid hush over the room, similar to the old days just before a felon was hanged at Tyburn. I could not believe my ears. Instinctively I tried mass-hypnosis in reverse, willing that somebody would bid and take the terrible burden from my shoulders.

"Two pounds!"

At last! Somebody had broken the silence with the most beautiful words in the world, and my frame visibly sagged with relief. The horrific picture entered my mind of Olga greeting me as she beheld a gigantic three-piece suite on the trailer, circa 1950 or Early Elizabeth the Second, well worn and de-sprung.

The hammer clacked down sharply on the rostrum and Mr Mellon did his *King Lear* piece about dying for shame over prices which did not even cover the cost of transport. "Sold to Mr Pook!" he barked to a black bundle of old clothes beside him which we recognized as Mr Benson, his aged clerk.

"Shold to Mishter Pook for two-pun, shir," Mr Benson confirmed, scratching the details in a ledger.

"Me!" I gasped.

Eddie Flaxmon, a third class bandit friend of mine, turned round in front of me. "Why did you bid against yourself,

Peter? Must be the Little Nells coming on."

The Little Nells was the trade term for those who had been in the business too long and were going off their rockers under its specialized stresses, like poor old Joe Thompson whose lifetime career of collecting harps had convinced him he was an angel—and Angel Gabriel at that—so that he appeared to float about his shop making conventional harpist movements with his hands. Just before he died he was planning to have the ceiling removed in order to facilitate his journey upwards to Heaven, but fate decreed he should depart through the front door like the rest of us.

"I must have had a mental blackout," I groaned. "I was so desperate to hear another bid that I gave it myself. Olga will kill me slowly when she hears."

"Ask Mellon to put the lot up again."

When Mr Mellon heard my plea he laughed that bitter mirthless laugh of auctioneers the world over. "You know the rules as well as I do, Mr Pook. Once the hammer has fallen the lot is yours, like a wife. The Law itself upholds your unassailable title to the goods. More than my job is worth to re-offer a lot. Next item please, porter."

You may cite dentists' and doctors' surgeries but nowhere do men sweat and tremble like in a sale-room. I was doing both, disastrous to concentration on my catalogue.

"Will you clear the lot for nothing, Eddie?" I begged.

"Sorry, pal. The settee frame is broken, the armchairs have got the sags, one wing is flapping and three springs are poking through. That apart, it would be a good buy for an enthusiastic upholsterer—for Bonfire Night."

"Do you think Wally would have it then?"

"He wouldn't touch it, Peter."

"Why not? He'd get it free."

"You know Wally. His big kick is the excitement of bidding."

"What, for one dollar!"

Now I was really snookered because Mr Mellon would not let you claim anything until you had cleared the junk. That was why there were so many Combined Lots in the catalogue to keep the rubbish moving, like this: 'Lot 897. One Pair of Early Victorian Ruby Glass Lustres *and* 20 Cans of Government Surplus Varnish *and* Considerable Quantity Rush Matting *and* Nearly Complete Set Flags of the British Empire'. In my previous business I took everything and tried to sell it, so that customers could come in and buy anything from a glass-cased specimen of a pouter pigeon to rolls of Pianola music. But in the back yard rotted the really unsalable debris, such as bamboo bookcases, cracked jardinieres, ancient radios and one odd ski. Paradoxically, I hid any good antiques which came my way and sold them to the trade, particularly the London dealers who visited me at least once a week in their ceaseless search for treasure. Much of this booty eventually ended up, via the dealer trade routes, in America, Canada, Switzerland and New Zealand.

My catalogue was visibly shaking as I forced my mind off three-piece suites and on the items which Olga had marked and pencilled in our top price, thus: 'Lot 635. 1850 Bentwood Rocking Chair with cane back and seat. £5 and not a penny more.'

This last remark was to curb my attacks of auction euphoria, whereby I became caught up in the feverish excitement of bidding under Mr Mellon's spell and would pay anything rather than be beaten. Such as when I had fought it out with some wealthy gentleman wearing a yellow turban and ended up as the owner of a hubble-bubble pipe and seven corrugated asbestos roofing panels and one chimney cowl, none of which I wanted, for £13. Even worse was my acquisition of a giant moose head with a twelve-foot antler span plus one elephant's leg umbrella-stand because Bernie Edelstein, chief nodder for the Ring, asked me for no apparent reason if my car was outside. I nodded that it was, whereupon Mr Mellon knocked down the game reserve lot to me for one shilling.

I concentrated desperately on the next item, Lot 137. Victorian Rosewood Davenport, Lined in Satinwood. Olga had marked the catalogue thus: 'Nice condit. No worm. Needs new lid hinge. Come in around £10 and go to £15. £18 max !!! then pull out.'

"Now, ladies and gentlemen, may I draw your attention to this delightful little Victorian escritoire in superb condition," Mr Mellon boomed, throwing his spectacles towards the object in question. "Who will start me at the ridiculous figure of £20?"

"Take a dollar, Guvner," Wally moaned from behind his cigarette end.

"Kindly ignore our friend wearing a cap and loin-cloth! Porters, hold up this beautiful little writing-desk so that people with money can see it."

Dutifully, two porters raised the desk on high—so high that we all stared upwards like some ancient tribe worshipping an idol.

"Woodworm underneath," Eddie Flaxmon remarked loudly to frighten Gentiles off.

"All right—a fiver," Bernie Edelstein called, as though he

sympathized with Mr Mellon and wished to help him out.

"Five pounds on my right," Mr Mellon announced as if we were all deaf. "Preposterous, but at least it's a start."

"I will tender a bid of six pounds," cried a Gentile lady wearing a floral hat, drop-earrings and butterfly glasses, nervously waving her catalogue at the rostrum.

This caused Bernie great distress. "Oh dear oh dear!—well, I'll go one more at seven. Yes, all right then, I'll risk seven. Seven quid."

"I hear a bankruptcy bid of seven pounds from my right. May we now stop acting and get down to business. Do I hear ten pounds from the floor?"

"Yes, ten pounds please," cried the nervous lady. "I have the exact spot in my extension lounge for that dear little davenport."

This was bad news because it meant we had a civilian on our backs who was so obsessed with the lot to the extent that she might be prepared to pay a fair price for it.

"Woodworm woodworm woodworm woodworm," mumbled the Ring worriedly.

"Eleven," Bernie grunted irritably.

The nervous lady ran Bernie up to nineteen pounds, then he triumphantly rounded it off at twenty while the lady, like many newcomers to auctions, had to be assisted to a chair like an unsuccessful gambler at roulette. My mind raced to calculate if Olga's £18 maximum would stretch as far as £21 under the stress of battle.

"Twenty-one!" I snapped before my mind had done its sum.

Mr Mellon was on it like a flash of lightning. "Twenty-five on my left!"

"Thirty," Bernie snarled.

"But I only bid. . . ."

"Thirty-five! Sold to Mr Pook at thirty-five pounds."

"Shold to Mishter Pook at firty-five-pun," echoed his clerk.

"But. . . ."

"You know the rules as well as I do, Mr Pook. After twenty we progress in fives."

So dismayed was I that I did what many men do who have given up smoking. I thrust a cigarette in my mouth, only to find one there already. I struggled to remember the rules but only one came to mind—that Mr Mellon went up in fives or tens whenever it suited him, which was pretty often.

"Oh the pain, oh the agony!" Bernie needled me. I ignored him in my struggle to collect my wits. Where, I asked myself, was the calm assured vendee that once I was? The catalogue informed me this was Friday, and not only Friday but also the 13th—and the *Daily Mirror* horoscope had already told me: 'Not the best day for business transactions, but watch out for affairs of the heart.' Well, my heart had been broken for a start. I had not fared so disastrously since Mr Mellon's Annual Farm Sale, where, owing to a printer's error in the catalogue, I thought I was bidding for horse brasses but was knocked down for a haywain and two horses.

My luck changed at Lot 149: Carved and Fluted Torchere on Tripod Base, 60 Inches High, circa 1845. Olga had marked this item: 'Sound condit. No worm. Top needs repolishing. Hide. £5 max.' Our code word *Hide* meant that the article was portable enough for me to conceal it from the crowd by arriving early and unobtrusively bunging it high up on the piles of furniture. Thus the torchere had escaped general notice and examination until it was offered for sale, when I would exclaim loudly, "Oh what a pity—riddled with woodworm!"

Then everybody would peer at the torchere and actually believe they could see the tiny holes themselves. Often Eddie Flaxmon would back me by observing, "Not for me, mate— the supporting dovetail-bracer's cracked right across."

By the time Wally Tate had put the mockers on the lot with "Take a dollar, Guvner," Mr Mellon was fighting to inject some motivation in the crowd to buy.

"Porter, kindly confirm that the torchere is free from woodworm, foot-and-mouth disease, dry rot and other imperfections so dreaded by our friends in the trade."

Henry the porter, whose low wages had imbued him with the spirit of truth seldom witnessed in ordinary men, donned his bifocals then grunted something which sounded like "Nes and yo," while he shook and nodded his head diagonally. The guiding principle of Henry's life was never to supply information gratis. His rate was a bob a nod, and those who tried to obtain it free discovered that he was deaf as he limped away from them hitching up his truss.

"Thank you, porter," Mr Mellon said disgustedly. "So now we know everything about the condition of this superb example of Early Victorian craftsmanship and the skilled use of carefully seasoned timber, may I ask for a starter of, say, ten pounds?"

"Take a dollar, Guvner."

"Ignoring the spendthrift representative of high finance in our midst, may I call for a realistic offer, please?"

"Would you consider my bid of five pounds perhaps, sir?" I inquired. This was my special creep bid I employed sparingly to keep in Mr Mellon's good books, because his sales were vital to our business, ensuring a permanent supply of stock which every dealer needs desperately.

Mr Mellon banged down the gavel immediately. "Sold to Mr Pook," he snorted.

I smiled at him gratefully. "Very much obliged to you, sir. Thank you."

"Crawler!" Bernie hissed, striking the item from his catalogue vehemently.

The lucky solo bid had come off, restoring my confidence as I glanced smugly at Bernie. "Technique," I replied, but I forgot about my rival because just behind him was standing the most beautiful blonde imaginable. She smiled at me with blue-black eyes, and I sensed she was gradually edging her way through the crowd towards me.

Naturally I was flattered, but being virtually woman-proof I was not unduly worried. With my iron resolution girls had often found me a bit of a heartbreaker, so I returned an inviting smile and edged towards her like a gentleman should. Although tall she contrived to look up at me appealingly, shaking back her hair which reached below her waist.

"Excuse me please, may I speak with you?" she whispered.

'At your service, miss," I simpered gallantly.

"This is my first, how you say, oxygen sale, and I am very nervous. Are you understanding my English?"

"I am understanding your English and now I am nervous too."

She laughed coyly, looking down at her long legs as I was doing. "You make fun. I see you win the torchere so boldly. You are experienced. You are man of the world."

"Nothing, nothing, my dear. Just luck, plus flair for the

game and years of practice." High cheek-bones, dimples and a cleft chin cut no ice with me, but talking to this female Viking certainly elated me.

"Forgive me, Mr Pork, my name is Tora."

"Hello Tora. My name is Pook, not Pork, but please call me Peter. Here is my business card."

"This card is calling you Nostalgia, yes?"

"That is just a trade name, dear. I am an antique dealer."

"You do not look antique to me, Peter, but quite young."

"I deal in antique furniture, Tora. Visit me any time."

"Ah, I am so lucky. You are antique dealer, so I ask you big favour. There is something I am wanting very very badly."

"Don't we all!"

"It is here in this catalogue book thing. See, Lot 167. Beautiful Wheilden Figure of Young Man. This I must take back for my collection in Norway. But too shy I am to speak out for it. You are professional buyer, Peter. Perhaps you will be so kind as to bid for me, yes?"

"Of course I will, Tora." Right now I would have done anything for her, let alone bid.

"Oh a million thank-you's, Peter; you are too kind. Naturally I will pay any commission fee you ask me."

"Let's say I'll do it for love, Tora—ha-ha-ha-ha!"

I was laughing inordinately because my eye had located Lot 167 in my own catalogue, which Olga had marked: 'Just the job. No chips or cracks. Go easy to £20.'

I have always despised weaker men who have made fools of themselves over women but this was a different kettle of fish, for I was simply extending courtesy to a visitor to our shores by combining business and pleasure.

31

"Do come see the lovely figurine, Peter. It is displayed in that glass cabinet," Tora coaxed. I found myself following her bust over to the display section, to view the Beautiful Wheilden Figure of Young Man.

"See how he is naked, Peter, showing us his splendid body," Tora squealled delighted.

"That's not all he's showing us either, dear."

"Oh, you naughty one! He is, how you say in English, he is making his water. Now, how you say in English what he is holding?"

"Holding his own?"

"Yes, he is holding his own pinnace for making his water."

I was disturbed to discover that during this conversation Tora was holding my hand.

"You see, Peter, this naked young man is standing on a beach and filling up the North Sea with his water. Such a lovely legend to tell us how the North Sea was formed."

"Last time I go swimming in it then, Tora."

"Ha-ha, you are so witty besides being such a clever man. What big fun it is to be with you, Peter. I forget everything."

I had forgotten everything too—especially Lot 162 : Three-Tier Regency Mahogany Whatnot with Pierced Brass Gallery and Brass String Inlay. 'Nice condit. Polish fair. Slight chip left front leg. Don't lose this for £20.'

Sweating and trembling like dealers do, I determined to find out what I had lost it for. Eddie flashed me his catalogue, where Lot 162 was recorded as going to Bernie Edelstein for £16. Guiltily I marked my own catalogue for Olga's audit later that day : 'The Ring took it for £26'.

"Why do you shake, Peter?" Tora asked, pressing close.

"Nothing, dear, only we must concentrate now because

your number is about to come up."

"Oh, such fun! You are going to try for my beautiful figure!"

"Not yet, dear—first I must bid for the Wheilden Young Man."

Despite my celibate nature and emotional steel I was not entirely immune to so much girl hanging on my every word and action. Tora had a disconcerting habit of laughing up into my eyes whenever either of us spoke, then snuggling her torso against mine. Other dealers cast envious glances at my predicament, noting my unusual lack of concentration, such as when I put the catalogue in my mouth and attempted to light it.

"How far will you let me go, Tora?" I whispered as Lot 167 arrived.

"As far as you want, you naughty agent!" she giggled.

"I mean what is your top price?—quickly, please."

"Just keep bidding, Peter. I want it so badly. If the price is too much I will squeeze you like this."

To my dismay Tora pinched my bottom so hard that my exclamation was interpreted by Mr Mellon as a bid, just as he accepted nods, winks, smiles, and even sneezes. In fact Ron Jones, who suffered a facial tic, invariably stood behind a furniture bay well clear of Mr Mellon's line of vision and shouted his bids for fear of being put out of business through overbuying.

"Ten pounds over there," Mr Mellon indicated with his outthrust spectacles. "Ah, one moment please."

The delay was caused by his clerk handing him a slip of paper which he scanned, then communicated to us. These mysterious messages invariably began 'I am instructed by my company to inform you that . . .' which puzzled me immensely because Mr Mellon was his own company, and the messages were written in his hand.

"Ladies and gentlemen, I am instructed by my company to inform you that Lot 167 has been amalgamated with Lots 168, 169 and 170 to form a combined Lot. Mr Pook, do you wish to withdraw your bid? You are on record in the past for complaining about Combined Lots."

"No, sir."

"Excellent. Your bid of twelve pounds stands. Do I hear thirteen? Yes, thirteen, fourteen, fifteen, twenty, twenty-five, thirty. . . ."

Events were racing ahead of my mind but Tora was pinching my bottom and at the same time urging me to bid.

"Thirty-five," I gasped.

"Forty, Mr. Pook. We're in tens now."

"Half a century," Bernie called for the Ring.

"Sixty," I shouted alarmed at the way Tora was pinching me and hissing "More, more, more!"

"Seventy."

"Eighty."

"Ninety."

"One hundred!" I cried, triumphant that mine was the rounding-off call. Bernie shook his head disgustedly.

"Sold to Mr Pook for one hundred pounds."

"Shold to Mishter Pook for one hun-pun," scratched the clerk.

"He's mine, he's mine!" Tora cried, holding me round the neck with both arms and dancing up and down.

"Lucky Peter," Eddie commented to the other dealers. "Wish I was hers."

"Thank you, thank you a million times, you wonderful man!" Tora kissed me, but I was scanning the catalogue over her shoulder and what I saw rapidly de-sexed me. 'Lot 168: 20 Ex-Army Meat Mincers. Lot 169: 6 Sacks Government Surplus Portland Cement. Lot 170: Ex-RAF Emergency Life Raft with Inflation Cylinder (Defective).' Some male instinct told me that Tora was unlikely to take these back to Norway with her Wheilden Figure.

I escorted Tora to the Bold Forester for vital stimulant and to explain the complexities of Combined Lots to an amateur.

"But, darling, these valuable things are for you," she replied according to form. "All I want is my beautiful Young Man holding his own pinnace and making his water to flood the North Sea so that our brave Vikings could sail to England and conquer the Englishmen."

"And I was the first one you met?"

"So these Combined Lots are my gifts to you for your kindness to me, Peter."

"Thank you, honey." Tora was so gorgeous that even cement and meat mincers seemed like lovers' gifts.

That same evening Olga and I sat down together with the catalogue and chatted over the day's events.

3

"So you met this dear old lady from overseas who asked you to bid for her on commission, Peter," Olga said during our routine auction post mortem. "Then you paid the bill for one hundred pounds in exchange for her cheque drawn on the Bank of Scandinavia."

"Correct, love."

"So she walks off with our Wheilden Figure, leaving you with just what we wanted to dress our windows in front of the Italian wall tapestries—six sacks of cement, twenty ex-army meat mincers and an inflatable life-raft. Perhaps we could display them tastefully laid out on this broken-down three-piece suite you purchased on the spur of the moment. All we need then to complete the window is an iron bed and a mangle."

"It's not been a good day, Olga. My horoscope said bad for business this morning."

"But favourable for flirtation."

"My head's too full of shop to bother about that, Olga."

She sighed heavily. "For goodness sake let's see what you netted on the credit side."

"Not our best day, Olga."

"Well, you got the torchere and that nice little Victorian mahogany teapoy on the tripod base."

"I did?"

"Did what?"

"Bought the teapoy."

"So the sale invoice says. Lot 177. Fifteen pounds."

"Oh yes, I remember now, Olga."

I thought desperately about the teapoy, which must have come up soon after Tora's figurine. Vaguely I recalled bidding almost by instinct, so befuddled were my wits. Now I knew I had been successful. Perhaps I was a better businessman drunk than sober, so to speak.

"Your horoscope also said you would receive tidings from abroad," Olga remarked.

"Expect that was the dear little old lady from Norway."

"You don't think this dear little old lady's cheque might bounce on you?"

"If you can't trust the Bank of Scandinavia who can you?"

"The dear little old lady?"

"Good as gold. I can read character."

"How is it there is cigarette ash smudged on this page of the catalogue, Peter? Does the old lady smoke?"

"Of course not, Olga. I lent it to Wally Tate for a few minutes. That's how the bottom came to be singed too." Life with Olga gave you the sharpest brain in the business.

"You forgot to kiss me when you came in, Peter. You can do it now if you like."

I kissed Olga rather quickly, breathing in as I did so.

"Why have you been smoking and drinking, Peter?" she asked.

"Popped into the Bold Forester for a snort because the sale had gone so badly, dear," I stalled, cursing my chlorophyll tablets for their ineffectiveness. "Then Eddie Flaxmon dropped his cigarettes over the bar and I accidentally put one in my mouth. Directly I spotted what I had done I spat it out."

"All twenty of them?' '

"Did you have better luck in the shop today, dear?" If ever the best form of defence is attack I needed it right now.

Olga's lovely face changed gear into a smile at last. "Mustn't grumble, Peter. Quite a few odds and ends as well as two big pieces. Sold the 19th-century French marble and spelter striking mantel clock to a complete stranger for eighteen guineas—cash, not a cheque. But the really exciting sell was that darling little George the Third sewing table in rosewood with inlaid floral decorations. I hated to part with it really, but who could refuse eighty guineas?"

"Eighty smackers! Well done girl! Who paid that amount?"

"Yosseff. Said he really bought it for me when . . . well . . . when I visit his palace one day."

"Yosseff! When you do visit his palace you'll certainly feel at home, dear. He must be furnishing it from us."

"Whom did the little old lady buy the Wheilden for, Peter?"

"Oh, her husband. He's mad about them. Wants the set."

"Odd! She's put her name and address on the back of the cheque as Miss."

"Perhaps they do that in Norway, Olga. Or maybe she's not so hot on her English." Or maybe Olga was the female successor to Sherlock Holmes, I thought to myself.

"How old would you say she was, Peter?"

"Oh, late seventies—even eighty. Used a stick," I replied confidently.

"Rather elderly to be a student. She's given her temporary

address as care of Cudford University. Unless she's studying Geriatrics."

"Maybe she's a lecturer there, Olga. Teaching Norwegian."

"Well, don't worry about it too much. We'll check up with Yosseff. After a year as a student he must know most of the staff there."

"Oh! Good idea, Olga."

"Yosseff may even recognize her perfume too—Estée Lauder. So clinging and distinctive."

I felt extremely tight about the neck, as if I needed fresh air—and solitude. "Well, Olga, enough of pleasure. I'd better run down to the Galleries and pick up the stuff so you can have your torchere and teapoy. They don't close till eight."

"OK, Peter, but don't go and pick up any stuff in the Bold Forester. Especially foreign stuff."

"Shan't be long, love. You can watch *The Mousetrap* on TV."

Because of Olga's warning about the Bold Forester I fell straight into the Flying Bull for vital resuscitation from Scotland, two doubles and a panatella, then hurried down to the Galleries. First I loaded the wrecked three-piece suite into the trailer. This is accomplished solo by dragging the settee on its end to the loading bay, then easing it into the trailer. Next, I carried each armchair upside-down on my head like an enormous bonnet. These I cradled in the settee. The survival raft fitted nicely on my roof-rack, followed by the meat mincers inside the estate car. Lastly, I carefully wrapped the torchere and teapoy with sacking to prevent chafing. Before leaving the sale room I tipped Henry, the porter, a dollar, as any wise dealer does whether he has earned it or not. Eddie told me this rule was even in the Bible as love thy porter as thy brother, though I could never trace the quote.

My first call, as has happened to many a dealer before and since, was to Cudford Refuse Disposal Tip, where I off-loaded the Elizabeth the Second Easy-Terms suite. I clung to the cement because everybody needs cement at some time or other, and no home should be without an ex-army meat mincer. I figured that eventually Eddie would take them off my hands for petrol money.

Arriving back at the shop in London Road and stopping only to admire my Nostalgia sign and Merrie England maypole, I started to off-load. First things first, Olga had schooled me, so I carried in the torchere and teapoy. Then the cement and mincers right through to the back yard before Olga saw them. It often occurred to me that if only I had another shop handy I could open as a general dealer. In fact, Olga sometimes worried that I had got junk in my blood and would never end up in Bond Street except with a barrow.

I hefted the life raft quite easily off the rack and across the pavement, but as I was squeezing through the door something caught against the handle. This was followed by a hissing noise quite alarming to hear, as if all four tyres on your car were going flat simultaneously. Nevertheless I freed the door handle of its impediment and negotiated the threshold, only to discover the raft had become too large for me to hold. It slipped from my grasp with a series of flop noises and began to open out like some science-fiction cushion in a nightmare.

There seemed to be rubber everywhere, growing before my eyes which could see that already the raft would not pass through the back door to the yard. To be honest I was not a little scared because I was covered and surrounded by canvas, deafened by the hissing and momentarily under the delusion that an elephant had got loose in the premises. The raft indeed seemed to be a living creature, flopping open and expanding so quickly that I was trapped in the shop.

I searched frantically for sign of the compressed-air cylinder that was activating the monster until I was sitting on the floor, jammed between that and the wall, convinced I had been sold a survival raft from a jumbo jet. Urged on by the noise of furniture overturning I scrambled underneath the raft where I located a box. Wrenching it open I discovered a complete survival kit of corned beef, condensed milk, tinned chocolate, shark repellent, sun lotion and a collapsible fishing-line, plus a desalination vessel for making fresh water.

By now I threw caution to the wind and shouted unashamedly to Olga for help. I heard her run downstairs, then her voice full of urgency.

"What's happened, Peter? Where are you? Good grief, I can barely open the door! There seems to be a giant balloon in the shop."

"Don't panic, dear, its only the survival raft. It's opened and blown itself up. I don't think it will get any bigger."

"That's because the shop won't let it. The thing's filled the place. My lovely shop is full of balloon. Oh dear oh dear oh dear!"

"Forget the raft for a minute, Olga, and help me, please."

"Where are you?"

"Underneath it."

"Then why don't you stop it wrecking us?"

"I can't locate the valve."

"What does it look like?"

"For heaven's sake fetch me a knife, Olga!"

"Oh why did you blow it up in the shop, you awful man?"

"Knife!"

When Olga returned with a knife she inched open the door, then screamed with shock because I was looking down at her from the ceiling. The only way I had been able to reach the door was to swarm up the loose canvas of the survival shelter aboard the raft, then squeeze along the ceiling like a giant fly. With wide eyes Olga thrust an arm through the aperture and handed me a pretty little Regency cake knife, as though we were on a picnic tea. It wouldn't even cut your finger.

"No good, Olga. Fetch me the big bread knife with the serrated edge. I've got to puncture the brute somehow. Bring my toolbox while you're at it. I may have to drill. I'll call it Operation Whale Fart."

"You don't have to be coarse as well as irresponsible."

As I waited on the ceiling above a shop full of inflated rubber the enormity of the situation struck me. The smell of stale rubber was appalling as I crawled along to inspect the front door. Peering down I could see it was still open, held thus by the body of the raft, some of which had actually bulged out onto the pavement. Fortunately the glass windows were safe because the rear wooden frames were taking the pressure, but the walls and ceilings were badly smudged with dirt and black from the vulcanized casing.

"Here you are, Batman," Olga called from the rear door. "Let's hope the shop doesn't sink when you puncture this thing."

I did not reply because I was reading. Sewn on the panel supporting me was an interesting piece of information headed: HOW TO INFLATE RAFT IN AN EMERGENCY. I read the instructions carefully, hoping to find something more pertinent to my predicament about how to deflate the raft in an emergency. Nothing.

"I'm terribly sorry about this little. . . ."

"Drop dead," Olga snapped, passing the tools up. "This could only happen to us—it's not even listed in the small print of our insurance policy, and that includes sonic bangs and landslides. Now get rid of this horrid thing." Her tone of voice indicated that I had brought home a dead rat or something.

As I made room to work by pressing my back against the ceiling a most alarming event occurred. The redistribution of weight on the bouyancy chambers triggered off the sudden activation of the blaze red self-erecting shelter canopy, so that a whole new world opened up and I tumbled into it like falling over the lip of a volcano. I found myself upside-down in a kind of rubberized marquee, while miscellaneous items essential to survival at sea deposited themselves around me, as if I had been running a stall at a fête until a truck backed into it.

I remember seeing a signalling torch, parachute distress flares, hand flares, a coiled rescue line, bellows, a repair kit, a first-aid box, sea-sickness tablets in tins, bulbs, batteries, a knife, two bailers, an Admiralty chart of the Pacific Ocean, an instruction manual, tin-openers, metal cups, plates and cutlery, a pair of paddles, and a leaflet entitled How to Swim.

"Peter, where are you?" Olga screamed.

A muffled cry from within the belly of the monster replied, "Don't be alarmed, dear. I'm down here in the self-erecting shelter canopy."

"What happened?"

"It self-erected itself and I fell in. I think I'm somewhere near the shampoo-basins we boarded over. There's enough stock down here to open another shop—a ship's chandler's." I added this last remark with some feeling as I extricated myself from the ropy octopus sailors call a sea-anchor.

I sat upright as soon as this was accomplished lest I should lose face in Olga's eyes. Not that she could see me but I always feared she might possess psychic powers like her dear mother, who was able to see right through walls, especially those of the Flying Bull Inn. Among my new stock was the fine Sheffield steel fishing knife capable of gutting a shark, so, armed with this weapon, I struggled to climb out of my trap with renewed confidence.

En route back to the ceiling I encountered another flag fastened to the fabric which read: 'DANGER! This raft inflates in one minute with high-compression CO_2 gas to a pressure of $4\frac{1}{2}$ pounds to the square inch'. Then it repeated the same good tidings in French and metric in case you were a Parisian antique dealer. The pressure was comfortingly low but I had read about carbon dioxide gas—or was the dangerous one carbon monoxide?—and wondered if Olga should phone the police to clear the area.

"Shall I phone for the fire-brigade, Peter?" Olga cried, proving she was psychic.

"No need, dear. I've decided to puncture it up front so the gas can go straight out into the street."

"Gas! Oh, this nightmare gets worse and worse. Don't you dare light a cigarette wherever you are."

Now I knew she was psychic because I was doing just that to steady my nerves.

"I'm warning you, Peter Pook, if you blow us up in our own shop I'll kill you!"

"It can't explode, Olga. CO_2 is an inert gas—that means it won't 'urt us. Ha-ha-ha-ha!"

"Stop your silly jokes and do something useful."

Armed with the knife and crawling along the ceiling towards our front door I became gripped by a primeval feeling that I was a Stone Age Man fighting a dinosaur inside a cave. The dinosaur had waddled into our home, and Olga was my Stone Age Woman urging me on to slay the beast. With a terrible atavistic roar I plunged the knife into the monster's head, shouting, "Take that, for wrecking my home and my life!"

I lay on the brute's body quite exhausted, listening to its breath ebb from its lungs with a satisfying hiss. "I've killed this dragon at last, Olga!" I yelled triumphantly, like a successful hunter.

"About time too, Saint George," Olga replied bitterly.

I don't remember any more.

When I awoke I heard the doctor saying to Olga, "A most unusual case, my dear, but what a blessing the shop door was open so that he fell out of the shop into the street as the caisson subsided. Otherwise his state of suffocation could have been fatal."

"Peter said the CO_2 gas was harmless, doctor. They were almost his last words."

"It is not poisonous, merely asphyxiating. I don't know what his trade is, Olga, but blowing up these enormous balloons in such a confined space is most inadvisable."

"He thinks he's an antique dealer. Nobody else does."

"Most odd!"

Olga insisted that I took things very easy during convalescence by staying indoors, particularly during opening hours at the Flying Bull, and redecorating the walls and ceiling of our showroom, plus repairing small structural damages caused by the raft. She had an obsession for business and a flair for doing it, dressing the windows with the cream of our objets d'art, telling me a dozen times a day, "Best side to London, Peter," to which maxim I never found a suitable reply.

A discreet notice in one window informed the public that cash was waiting inside for all kinds of merchandise from yesteryear which at present was lying unprofitably in their attics and cellars where we could not get our hands on it. Olga also advertised in the local Echo newspaper; genteel ads which began: 'Lady would like to purchase privately. . . .' These two sources provided a good part of our stock, such as chaise-longues at an average price of £5, and Pembroke tables of various periods averaging £10, and small Moorish coffee tables at £1. Olga had a penchant for swing toilet mirrors, Victorian or earlier, some with barley twist supports, some in narrow mahogany, usually keeping about half a dozen in stock.

Looking back, some of the prices seem quite ridiculous today, such as Victorian beechwood stretcher table for £2, a Victorian burr walnut round table, eighteen inches across, on a spiral twist column and tripod legs for £2 15/-. A round Victorian dining table on a single column with tripod base for £5. A fine Georgian writing-bureau, four drawers, brass handles and let-down top for £30. Everything seemed to be relatively cheap and in plentiful supply. Even round three-tier mahogany dumb waiters of the George the Fourth and William the Fourth periods were to be had around £15. Victorian and Edwardian revolving piano stools in mahogany or rosewood were standard price at £1, and the endless supply of two-tier plant stands from the same periods we bought for shillings, often as low as two shillings.

On our time off, Olga and I spent most of our leisure browsing round curiosity shops in other areas, always on the look out for booty, as we called it, seldom returning without a cache of oddments from other dealers. One of the joys in this trade is buying from one another, and we certainly had our share of professional visitors. Most of them were searching for general bargains but we also had the specialists, characters who came in hunting for their particular line. A man—or woman—might want only tiles, or glassware, or china. A friend of ours wanted harpsichords and spinets, another spent his time in the quest for spittoons and chamber pots, another would look at nothing but early surgical instruments. One specialist concentrated on paintings, while yet another sought only grandfather clocks.

We grew to know and like them all, for surely a man whose sole passion in life is old watches, or harps, or warming-pans, cannot be all bad.

Lower down the pecking order came Mr Francis, who drove up every few weeks to see if we had any feather beds for him at thirty bob a time; and Mr Clough whose mission involved scrap metal, particularly brass, copper and pewter. Whatever you can think of, someone's career is collecting it, from old coins to old postcards, and all these perks of the trade mounted up to pay our petrol bills and other sundries. Nor was Olga averse to leaving the shop when she heard the cry of the rag-and-bone man outside just in case he had some rarity among his rubbish.

I had already established a small workshop at the rear for

47

washing and minor repairs. When you purchase a load of
china and glass from an old house, say a tea-chest full or
more, it comes in brown—or even black—and must be carefully washed and cleaned out before it can be displayed, turning white in the process. We used a weak solution of Lux in
warm water for this purpose, with various brushes, tooth-
brushes and pipe-cleaners to reach into crannies. To scour
the bottoms of long thin vases, otherwise inaccessible, we
employed tiny airgun pellets and detergent, shaking vigor-
ously to remove the residue of time.

Much of the furniture we carefully washed with warm
Lux, gradually soaking away the grime of years and the marks
of use until a near black piece of furniture would change
miraculously back to the pristine golden brown of the original
timber. When the piece was dry we used various polishes and
waxes to nourish the wood and make it sparkle for our display
windows.

Rather like a dry-cleaner, I became quite expert at eradicat-
ing blemishes from furniture, from a two-hundred-year-old
grease spill to modern ink stains. For this purpose I built up
an assortment of gentle abrasives and solvents, learning that
most marks could be gradually coaxed away without damag-
ing the patina. I taught myself how to effect simple repairs
to woodwork and metal, but the art of French polishing
evaded me. Fortunately I knew an ancient French polisher,
Mr Bentley, reputed to have retired before the Second World
War and who was more familiar with the Boer War, who
delighted in helping me out. If a table top was in poor condition I had only to transport it to his house and call for it a
week later, when he had transformed it into a gleaming mirror
exactly matching the base. For this service he charged me

beer money, and I secretly prayed that God would make an exception of Mr Bentley as a reward for his craftsmanship by never letting him die.

At the other extreme young Vic Armstrong, still in his twenties, undertook our upholstering work, refurbishing settees, sofas and chairs as good as new. I could not estimate how many chaise-longues he resprung and recovered in Regency stripe fabrics of golds, creams and wines when the chaise-longue leapt back into public favour. Although Vic loved his craft he also loved money, collecting the furniture in his van and often returning it the same day.

Woodwork damage beyond my small ability we put out to Gus Piper, the local carpenter and joiner who proved to be a cabinetmaker also. His skill was such that I felt I was a child who had found a chisel and was playing with it as a toy. Then Gus knew a good glazier, Tom Roach, who could replace cracked or missing glass, and Mr Bentley knew Alf White who could cut plate-glass mirrors to any size and through any curvature. We did a nice line with Alf White, for when we bought a lot containing old gilt picture-frames he turned them into mirrors—and nothing sells like an old gilt mirror. Nor must I forget Mr Bloomfield, the watchmaker and jeweller a dozen doors down from us, who repaired anything up to a grandfather clock for us, making missing parts on his tiny lathe.

This pool of skill and craftsmanship was invaluable to us because no longer did everything we purchased have to be near perfect. We were able at last to buy damaged objets d'art on the cheap, secure in the knowledge that we had the means to resuscitate them to first-class selling condition. This opened up to us a whole new world of stock sources, and later on we went so far as to start a small repair service for customers' own possessions. I suppose the furthest extension of our service was best exemplified when I visited a lady's house in order to treat her staircase for woodworm. While working on the job I spotted there in the hall a late eighteenth-century longcase clock with an enamel face in an oak case by Jos Melchett of Southampton. I shed a few tears and she let me have it for £10. Furthermore, she was so pleased I had saved her staircase that she presented me with the cup she gave me coffee in—a Victorian moustache cup.

Following my inviolate rule I carted my treasures away with me, the cup in my pocket and the clock on my back, safe from those two menaces to our profession, greedy relations and nosy neighbours.

When I reached base to lay the booty at Olga's feet she praised me and patted my head—then handed me the note about the oil-painting.

4

The case of the oil-painting has been so publicized by the press that I have not written about it till now. The note merely contained the woman's name and address, a gipsy-looking type of woman according to Olga, so off I went like a good dealer. One followed up every lead because if the main chance was unsuitable there were often other perks to be gained in the same house. I always scanned the place, paying special attention to mantelshelves and china-cabinets in case they held lustres, figurines, pair of hands, glass paperweights and similar prizes.

Mrs Kendal's residence was not very big, being one of those early trailers which developed from the caravan. However, it was neat and clean, pleasantly situated amid trees and bordered by a low privet hedge. Washing hung on the line and chickens scattered as I walked up the garden path.

The lady who opened the front door was extremely petite and pushing sixty. She asked me inside, then produced a pot of tea as if by magic. "I couldn't bring the picture along to your shop, Mr Pook, because it's too big and heavy for a little 'un like me," she explained, pouring tea, "but as you can see for yourself, what good is a picture that size in my place?"

"Turn your unwanted possessions into hard cash, Mrs Kendal," I replied, quoting from our ad. Even as I spoke my eyeballs automatically revolved as I cased the joint for bric-à-brac.

"But before you look at it let me tell your fortune, sir," she smiled. Without warning she lifted her long skirt right up revealing a red underskirt decorated with playing cards, undoubtedly a complete pack.

"They call me Gipsy Kendal round these yere parts, sir, for 'tis true there's Romany blood in me veins from somewheres, though God knows where. I bin reared in these yere parts girl and woman I 'ave, and ever since I can remember I've had this gift with the cards like, lookee. You arst anyone within ten miles and they're tell 'e the same, that I tells the cards and I tells 'em true. Oh sir, I should love to tell yourn for you got a lucky face if ever I seed one. Just move your cup over a wee bittie so I can lay the cards for 'e, sir."

Experienced dealer as I was, I felt taken aback by this novel approach to business but I could not refuse because the cards were being laid in front of me as I sat with my mouth open.

"Oh sir, I sees good fortune and money and romance and ambitions realized and splendid health for 'e already, sir," Mrs Kendal gasped, as though this was merely the trailer for wonders to come—so far there were only five cards down.

"I sees you are a business gentleman, sir, and your work will thrive and prosper for you under the ace o' diamonds, sir. And here comes success in love and marriage under the queen o' hearts' sir. My, yourn a lucky 'un, you be! And here be money to the house, sir; a great deal of money—perhaps you do's the football pools, sir. That kind of money. Bless me, there's no stopping it, for here as large as a house comes your health cards—not your National Health cards, sir, ha-ha-ha—for a long life, strong as a horse and fit as the

Devil hisself. What's this I sees? A dark woman loves 'e, sir, but beware of a fair woman to the house; a fair woman who has taken a long journey across the sea. My word, how the women love 'e, sir. You're Fortune's favourite child, sir. . . ."

I sat there smugly pleased, my belief in the occult now confirmed beyond doubt as the old lady poured out the truth about my life and character. When at last she finished I asked to view the picture, which she produced wrapped in sacking from beneath her bed. Framed in gilt, the painting measured some five feet by three on my tape. It was grimy and obviously old.

" 'Tis a pretty farmin' picture, sir, lookee," Mrs Kendal explained, in case I failed to recognize cows in a meadow.

"And the milkmaids going to milk," I confirmed.

"Not before time, sir, judging by the size o' they udders."

"And the cows are bursting too."

"I calls it Milk-O, sir."

"Who wouldn't?"

"I expects you thinks it be dirty, sir."

"Oh, I'm as broad-minded as the next man."

"For it has lain under my bed ever since I can recall, sir."

"Do you know who painted it, Mrs Kendal?"

"Why bless you, sir, my late husband Billy always said 'twas done by his great-grandfather, Willie Kendal. So 'twas he would never part with 'un, lookee."

This was bad news because family heirlooms sent the price up. "How much will 'e take for 'un, Mrs Kendal?" I found the lady's broad dialect most contagious.

Mrs Kendal smiled as though I was simple-minded. "Why bless 'e, sir, ten pun o' course. My Billy always said 'twas worth ten pun, nor would 'e take a penny more nor a penny

53

less. He did tell me he heard his own grandfather say how his father did say 'twas worth ten pun o' anybody's money—so ten pun it be."

"Suppose I gives 'e five pun for 'un, Mrs Kendal?"

"Then shall I still be holding me hand out for the other five pun, sir. Billy always told me that when 'un names a price 'un mun't come down—nor go up neither."

"Will 'e meet me then at seven pun ten, Mrs Kendal?"

"Tell 'e what I'll do, sir. If you do give me a pun for telling your lucky cards, sir, I'll meet e' at nine pun."

"So how much actual cash do I have to give 'e?"

"Ten pun, sir."

I handed over two fives and asked Mrs Kendal to sign the receipt—which was a mistake in itself.

"Bless 'e, sir, I am but a poor country woman who can neither read nor write. What I always do's, sir, is to make me mark."

"You've certainly made your mark on me, Mrs Kendal, especially when it comes to fixing a price."

Mrs Kendal put her nose to the paper, tongue out, as if she was creating a new design for currency notes, then drew the most laborious X I have ever witnessed. After all, you only have to draw a line, then cross it with another one. As was my rule, I departed the moment the ink was dry, for customers have a habit of changing their minds at the last moment, or being tortured by conscience, or—in one instance —receiving an urgent spirit message from the other side that Great-grandma was doing her nut up there demanding a cancellation of the deal.

Olga was quietly horrified that I had paid £9 for a picture— I maintained a discreet silence about the fortune-telling—

which would probably end up as one more gilt mirror from the frame. Neither of us knew much more about paintings than the ability to distinguish between oil and water-colour so Olga had the bright idea of including our acquisition in Mr Mellon's Art Auction, which he held on the first Monday of every month.

"At least we might get our money back with a bit over for our expenses and Mr Mellon's commission," Olga decided.

"Yes, dear, and I'll put a £15 reserve price on it in case Wally walks in there by accident and offers a dollar." I sensed Olga was keen to out the picture because she considered it to be slightly rude. We had a small replica of the statue of *David* in the window, and she had hung the price tag so carefully that it served as a kind of fig-leaf.

I drove down to the sale-room, duly entered the painting, then forgot all about it. I'll tell you why I forgot all about it—in fact I'll tell you why I forgot about everything just then.

Olga had made me sign the pledge that not another cigarette should ever touch my lips—had me swear it on the Bible and actually sign a written statement. Thereafter I gave much thought as to how one might smoke a cigarette without employing the lips, such as up the nose, or, more practicable, through a cigarette-holder. Eventually I decided to cultivate the pipe image as the only escape clause worthy of a gentleman, which gave me a new hobby.

Very soon I possesed five pipes, from the standard wooden variety right through the species to a metal pipe reminiscent of our plumbing system. My accessories grew daily until it became necessary for me to use a document wallet as a kind of hand-bag to carry the equipment about with me. My learner's kit comprised a tobacco-pouch, slice of potato for moisture, pipe-cleaners, matches and gas-lighter, a bowl reamer, cleaning tissues and a smoker's penknife. This latter instrument was a handy all-purpose tool containing four gadgets, such as a tamper and stem-rodder. I discovered that a pipe had one great advantage over cigarettes in that it lasted far longer. On the debit side I learned that trying to light a pipe whilst driving sent the car off the road, and suspicious holes appeared in my sweaters and trousers.

Having deposited the painting safely I repaired to the Wooden Indian Cigar Store to purchase a sixth pipe, a revolutionary model with a meerschaum bowl, two filters, an anti-dottle barrier valve, windshield, a great deal of aluminium plumbing and a non-slip mouthpiece, while underneath was a tiny drain-cock. It reminded me of an early motor-cycle.

I retired to the privacy of Cudford Station's waiting-room to run in my new model with two fills, then, slightly dazed, I strolled round the block to rinse my mouth out with fresh air before returning to the shop. Those were the days you may have read about when it was still possible to park outside your own premises without being ticketed, fined and towed away. From the car I could see into the shop. Olga was talking to a customer whose back was to me but it was obviously a gorgeous blonde on stiletto heels in a green dress. Spotting the car, Olga hipped out and said to me in her church service voice, "There's a lady to see you, Peter. A dear little old lady. A dear little old lady from Norway—all five-foot-eight of her."

"To see me, dear?"

"Something tells me she hasn't come to see me."

"What ever can she want with me?"

"You would know that better than I do. I'm not a man. Ostensibly she is looking for statuettes and figures—yours, I shouldn't be surprised."

"Did she say she knows me, dear?"

"Only by cheque, Peter. She thinks you're Wonderman. Show her that *David* and tell her it's you on bath night."

"I'm so busy right now, dear. Couldn't you handle her, please?"

"No, Peter, you must face up to your responsibilities. You handle her—that's obviously what she wants."

"Well, I have to be nice to our clients, Olga."

"Don't be too nice to this one. She's the type who'll ask you to show her a chaise-longue, then tell you the job is getting on top of her."

"Olga! I've never heard you speak like that before."

"Because I've never seen a female like her before, Peter. She makes your last girlfriend look like a little old man."

I entered the shop and made polite greeting noises at Tora. Before I could put the counter between us she came very close, holding my jacket lapel with two fingers like a tailor and brushing me with her bust. Fortunately my cast-iron will and Olga's proximity made me immune to silly feminine wiles as I fought to concentrate on business.

"So you have come at last, you lovely man," Tora purred, talking into my eyes. "How I have missed your witty tongue and your vast experience since last you were bidding for me at the auction, darling. Do have a cigarette, my clever agent."

"No thank you, Tora, I've given it up," I laughed gaily, pushing away the gold case of fifty king-size.

"Given it up! So soon! How strong you must be to cut off in such short time since we were together."

I was sweating because although Olga had retired discreetly to our room behind the shop we had replaced the door by a curtain, making it easy for her to give me the big ear unseen. I had done it myself when Yosseff was trying to buy Olga for Oil-land.

"What can I do for you today, Tora?" I whispered.

"First I come to see my lovely man who took such care of me at the sale, darling. Second I come to ask about any more figures like my lovely man holding his pinnace to flood the North Sea."

"May I show you *David* in the window?" I extracted the replica from the window, quickly removing the price tag lest Tora should think it obstructed the view.

Tora fondled the white marble with long fingers. "Oh this I am liking, Peter. It is a trifle small but the detail is so exquisite, right down to the tiny veins. To me this is you standing at the auction with no clothes on. How much is it costing to add to my collection?"

I scanned the simple code we used on the tags, whereby we were able to adjust the price according to the customer. For example, when Lady Erge came in I always added fifty per cent to allow her to beat me down to ten per cent above the price so she could tell her friends what a bargain she had won. You had to add on a bit for dealers too, so that there was room for manœuvre when they asked for the knock off. When one particularly tight trader visited us I used to hide, then call out, "There's no-one here, so you can steal it and run off."

"For you I can do it for £16, Tora," I whispered.

"Do what, you naughty boy?" she giggled. "And why

have you lost your voice—is it because we are so close together?"

"The price of the statuette is £16, Tora. Excuse me." I made the last remark because Tora had actually squeezed into the window with me. It was the small side window reserved for glass, plate and similar small items, so that to the passers-by who stared at us we must have resembled two giants in a china-cabinet. Now I dared not move an inch in any direction among the packed display, being compelled to stand frozen like a tailor's dummy with one arm outstretched.

"Back out of the window, Tora, *please*," I begged. "I'm wedged in and daren't move."

Tora giggled. "Am I being naughty, Peter? Never before have I stood in a shop window."

"Never before have I been through one. Let me out before we have an accident."

"Now we are so close and you cannot retreat, yes?"

"Not without claiming on our glass insurance."

"I expect you would like to kiss me and tear my clothes off and—how you say in English—rubbish me."

"In a shop window!"

"Well, if you do I cannot resist you. How can a mere girl stop such a bull of a man from rubbishing her in a china shop? She is defenceless against his insatiable lust. I shall be brave—I shall not scream for help."

"I shall. Please move back, Tora. Olga's window is sacred. She even flicks the spiders out."

"You must know, Peter, that I am art student. You see, I need a model of a man. A man like you. I should very much like to make an example of you. You will stand naked in the window and I shall call it 'The Bull in a China Shop'.

Under my hand you will be immortalized for all time in cement."

"Cement!"

"Yes, my medium is cement. It used to be mud but that is not hard enough. A strong man like yourself needs cement. See how beautifully you pose, Peter—you have not moved for several minutes. Perfect."

"I dare not. One mistake in here costs pounds."

"So drop round tonight about eight, Peter. Here is my card. Then you can come out of the window."

I assented to the proposition not only because I was getting cramp but also because Olga had emerged to arrange the flowers. Worst of all, she was singing gaily and when Olga sang gaily all was not right with the world, being more in the nature of a bird's territorial call, warning intruders that they would be defeathered. She was one of those delightful old-fashioned maidens who believed in one man to one woman, and the place for any interloper was on the floor with her throat cut.

"Promise, Peter?" Tora said, heaving her bosom. Heaving her bosom took on a new meaning when Tora did it, so that I was driven to promise by a speechless nod. Olga told me later that Tora was almost wearing a jade green halter-neck dress, though not so much a dress as a clever device to prevent her appearing topless in public. The wall side of the window was mirrored to reflect and enhance the goods, and when I saw the gold and green image of this leggy doll full-length in the pier-glass I lost some of my ice-cold frigidity to the extent that several red twist-stem wine glasses commenced to tinkle embarrassingly on their shelf. Even the window was beginning to steam up.

I gave Olga a confident glance to let her see I was as impervious as ever, and that I was merely being nice to customers for trade purposes. After all, many lonely women came to our shop more for company and chat than business, though usually they did purchase, albeit very slowly.

I wrapped *David* three times, having accidentally packed my thumb with it on two occasions, then found I had a surplus of receipt bills for the sale—five in all—one of which recorded that *David* had sold Tora to me. Olga was hovering in the background, humming gaily as she adjusted wall mirrors to one thou. of an inch. Always an ominous sign when Olga went onto mirrors because she could see everything as well as hear—even what I was thinking.

Calmly, debonairly, I took Tora's twenty pounds and gave her sixteen pounds change, which she kindly returned so I could reduce it to four. Laughing delightedly at my little mistake I opened the door for her, following closely after to deliver *David* safely to her car.

"Oh, I have not brought the car, darling," Tora smiled, tossing back the long tresses. "Still much shopping to do, so please bring the parcel with you tonight. Remember?" Wrinkling her nose and kissing mine she wiggled off.

I returned to the shop trying to hide *David* behind my back, a futile deception in a place so well equipped with mirrors. I realized this when I saw Olga staring at three reflections of me holding a brown parcel behind my back, so instinctively I held it in front of me.

Now Olga was a beautiful saint of old as depicted by Titian, grieving over the ways of men yet radiant through spiritual strength. She was too busy dusting to speak.

"Well, that was a good sell, outing *David* like that," I

61

said casually.

"Yerse." It was one of Olga's longer yes's, slightly shorter than a sentence.

"You know I'm not interested in the girl herself, Olga."

"Yerse."

"After all, I'm a man of the world, not one of your weaklings who make fools of themselves at the sight of a pretty ankle."

"Pretty ankle! She was showing a pretty everything."

"So I was just tagging her along to make the sale, Olga."

"Yerse."

"Some women never give up, Olga. They can see I'm rock yet they think they can vamp me with the old come-on. Doesn't it make you sick?"

"Yes you do."

"I mean doesn't it make you sick of your own sex, Olga?"

"No, Peter—yours."

"All I can say is I hope I never see the doll again."

"Then you'd better shut your eyes when you deliver the goods tonight. Salaam and greetings, your royal highness!"

Olga's welcome and change of expression was prompted by the entry of Yosseff behind my back, excessively handsome in a white turban and matching teeth. He fired his knock-out smile at Olga. "Ah my pretty one, you must not address me thus. Apart from my palace and my lands I am an ordinary run-of-the-mill prince. Often do I wish I was just a humble student existing on an allowance from his father of a miserly million pounds or less. Money can bring great unhappiness."

"Depends whose it is," I laughed. "Only other people's makes me unhappy."

"Quiet, Peter," Olga snapped. "I'll attend to Yosseff while you ponce yourself up as the delivery boy. Now, Yosseff is my ideal of a real man."

Yosseff's lighthouse mouth flashed teeth. "Ah my lovely one, you say I am pretty because you like to flatter me with the truth. You must come with me to Makara soon, for you are a beautiful strong woman who will bear many sons."

"Really, Yosseff, you shouldn't speak like that, especially in front of Peter," Olga chided him delightedly.

"Of course, all I can offer you is position, riches and a palace. There will be also servants, cars, your personal swimming-pool, horses—enough for your everyday needs."

Olga seemed quite impressed so I did not counter with what I could offer her—which she knew anyhow. "How shall we get there, Yosseff?" she sighed.

"You must be satisfied with my own executive jet. It is fast, it is safe, it is better than nothing."

"Can Peter come with us, Yosseff?"

"Can Peter come with us, my pretty one? What better than Peter come with us? But I cannot guarantee his safety. He may become lost in the desert where so many men die of thirst. My country is most dangerous for white men. As your wonderful Noel Coward is singing, 'Mad dogs of Englishmen go out in the midday sun without their titfers on'. Then they drink too many sundowners and bite each other. It is not a good place for a white man. We have lost so many of them through drink, drugs, heat, snake-bites and fighting. Others cannot survive without their beloved telly box and go stark raving mad."

"Perhaps I should stay home and cook the lunch," I

suggested.

"Oh that would be fantastic, Yosseff!" Olga cried. It was remarkable how I had this power to become invisible at times, when people could neither see nor hear me. I chuckled and waved my arms in gesture but they seemed to think I had gone through the floor.

"What I have come to visit you about, my beautiful one, is to select some gift worthy of your loveliness that you would like to find in your boudoir when you arrive."

"Oh Yosseff, you really mustn't!"

"What I had in mind—with your permission—is that Regency gold leaf convex mirror to reflect your beauty."

"A convex mirror distorts beauty," I interrupted brightly. "Makes your face look like a frying-pan."

"Oh Yosseff, if I am worthy of such a gift I should prefer the one next to it. The George the Third mahogany fret mirror with carved and gilded birds."

"And it costs more too," I observed.

"For you, my sweetness—anything. Of course, how stupid of me. That is the one you shall have. Money is no object when your happiness is involved."

I walked right round the shop to check if I was visible on the move but apparently not. I hopped over to the mirror in question to scan the price-tag. "Thirty-five pounds means that my happiness is involved too. Of course it is, Peter. It really is a gorgeous mirror, Olga. Yes, Peter, it happens to be my favourite. Lucky you, Olga, having Yosseff buy it for you. . . ."

Embarrassed, I put my hand over my mouth to stop talking to myself but it was unnecessary because nobody seemed to hear me. Silently I folded my tent and stole away, feeling like the Invisible Man with chickenpox. Collecting the parcel of *David* on the way I anticipated that Tora would find me a much more solid proposition.

5

I sat in the waiting-room of Cudford Station contentedly smoking my new pipe; running it in, as I liked to think of it. I favoured the station because I dared not smoke at home and I never mastered the art of smoking outdoors. Nor was it permitted in Cudford Library, where I often passed an exciting hour reading my own novels.

Another reason for my sitting here, waiting for the clock to register seven-forty-five so I could call on Tora, was that my argument that the cessation of cigarette coupons would prevent us getting our home together had cut no ice with Olga. On my lap reposed my new tobacco handbag, now complete with tissues, two packets of pipe-cleaners of different gauges, wool; one packet of pipe-cleaners, nylon, for scouring; a tin of smokers' tooth-powder; a portable ash-tray for use when visiting folks who did not indulge and had also blocked up their fireplaces; and finally, for emergencies in the home—such as at midnight in the toilet—a tin of snuff. Frankly, there was also a dummy cigarette made of plastic, blackened at one end where I had tried to light it so often, but I never used this lately because its psychological purpose of soothing the addict tended to drive me off my rocker. To counteract this I always carried a packet of anti-smoking tablets and a case of miniature cigars.

I sat there happily puffing away at my new patent pipe, all systems go, reading the cigarette advertisements through the waiting-room windows and pondering whether I was suffi-ciently experienced yet to invest in a Dunhill. On the quarter hour I ran nonchalantly over to the car and drove to Tora's address.

Fortunately she was a non-resident student at Cudford University, living in a mews flat at the arty end of town—cobbles and gaslamps format—down a cul-de-sac called Old Carriage Way. One gained admittance by striking a hanging iron serpent with a panel-beater's beetle or maul, which resonated at middle C, so Tora explained later.

There was Tora within, welcoming me as though I had returned from a lifetime in China. She kissed me, simul-taneously flipping open the gold case of fifty king-size, re-minding me of an accordion keyboard. I took one to be sociable, then tried to sit down on the black bean-bag settee without appearing to have fallen from the ceiling. My greatest difficulty was leaning back in sophisticated pose without slowly performing a neck roll onto the carpet behind. Three times I had to return and apologize for somersaulting during conversation.

"This smock I am wearing is my peignoir, darling," Tora explained, seeing my eyes widen every time she moved. "I wear this because I am an artist and an artist must be free. Free to move, free to create, free to express, free to make love."

"It's certainly free and easy," I agreed lamely. If the peig-noir was any freer it would have made a good headscarf.

"How are you liking my collection, darling?" Tora in-quired, drawing my attention to one wall entirely shelved with nude young men and boys in the act of flooding oceans, lakes, fountains and even buckets. "I expect you can guess

67

what my hobby is, yes?"

"Irrigation?"

"Ah my Peter, how witty you are!"

"Well, it's a hobby that will never dry up on you, dear."

"*David* will go here in this special section because he is just standing there not really doing anything in particular."

"Perhaps he needs a drink to make his eyes water."

"Ah, I can take a hint, Peter. Let me give you some saki."

While Tora poured the saki I listened to mood music from the gram. She was playing a vintage seventy-eight of Layton and Johnson singing *Love Me Honey-Chile*, circa 1926, and I wondered if I could make her an offer for the disc to sell in our shop.

I sat there smiling cynically, like Casanova in a strip-club, amused by the way this naïve girl was trying to woo me on the femme fatale formula of the old pre-war movies. After 'Come up and see my etchings' she was exploiting soft music and liquor. If the next move was 'I'll just slip into something more comfortable' the only thing left after the peignoir would be for her to slip into bath water. How ingenuous did she rate me? The whole routine was so passé that I chuckled derisively—so derisively that once more I rolled backwards off this cursed bean-bag settee with no guts.

Drink in hand Tora leaned towards me, smiling into my eyes intensely. "Oh how you do inspire me, Peter!" she gasped, as if she had been running. I wished she would not keep paying me this compliment because she put so much feeling into each word that a lot of her tended to burst from the peignoir like Aphrodite rising from the sea. She certainly presented an impressive argument against unisex, I thought to myself as I wiped a little saki from my lap. For some unaccountable reason my left hand was shaking, so I transferred the glass to my right hand, whereupon that hand threw the remainder of the liquid into my face.

To marshal my thoughts I checked the time. Opposite me was a large statue of Apollo wearing only a fig-leaf and even that was twined in his hair as he looked down to contemplate the clock his hand was holding. It registered just after nine.

"Why are you staring at his clock, Peter?" Tora giggled.

"I stare at everything here—it's so unusual."

"But of course. Tonight I have several unusual things to show you."

"You've certainly shown me all the usual things, dear."

"Before supper I want you to take the sauna bath, Peter. I want you to feel as you have never felt before."

"But I do already."

"Remove all those unhealthy trappings of decadent society. Take your clothes off and rise up against stifling tradition."

"Sorry, Tora, that's going too far. Count me out, please."

Was it possible that a doll could be so pathetically obvious in this day and age of equality of the sexes and the disappearance of mystery in women with the girlie magazines full of pictures like butcher's meat charts. I laughed sardonically at such futile subterfuge on Tora's part.

The sauna was the new Home Steamer model installed in your ordinary household bath, ideal for flat dwellers short of room for a log-cabin. I sat in the bath really steamed up, my pores open like woodworm holes as the sweat ran out. After some ten minutes the bath emptied of itself like a launderette machine, then cold water flooded in. So cold that tiny ice-cubes rushed through in the water, causing me to turn from red to blue in seconds and so invigorating that I screamed like a frightened schoolgirl.

"Are you all right, Peter?" I heard Tora call from the kitchen. I tried to answer no, but my larynx was too frozen to vibrate. Worse still, my limbs refused to obey urgent brain messages to leap out of the bath. I lay there without sensation, numb and marble-hard like a frozen duck in the supermarket. Round my neck ice was forming, gradually spreading over the entire surface of the bath—so that I appeared to have emerged from an ice-hole like a Polar seal. I sensed that my body was turning into a statue, similar to a rabbit stiff in a deep-freeze. As far as I was capable of discerning my lungs had stopped breathing.

Again without warning the bath emptied itself, making me wonder if I should next be given the first rinse cycle before being spin-dried. In fact I did lie there as lifeless as the week's washing except that I was surrounded by ice fragments. When Tora entered she found me with one leg over the edge of the bath, whereupon she rolled me over to drop on the carpet. Then she semed to go berserk, beating my body with a bush.

"I am beating you with this hard bush to give you the complete sauna, Peter," she cried.

"I didn't think you were dusting me with talc powder," I gasped.

"This will improve your circulation and increase your virility."

"You could have fooled me, Tora. You're flogging a dead horse."

"Now turn over so I can do your front."

"Have mercy—please!"

I squatted crosslegged on the floor of the lounge wearing

my new sauna shirt. Tora told me supper was ready but I obviously was not. I was trembling all over to the extent that it worried me that my body was beginning to hum. Tora was kind enough to hold the glass of scotch to my lips but even so it seemed that the simple operation of drinking would break either the glass or my teeth.

"First we enjoy the delicious Finnish dish of hernekeitto, Peter," Tora enthused, placing a bowl in front of me. The bowl was an exquisitely shaped replica of the little boy at the fountain in Brussels—the famous Mannekin-Pis.

"What is it, Tora?"

"Pea soup—ha, ha, ha, ha! Hernekeitto, Finnish pea soup."

"Ask a silly question. . . ."

"This is containing pig belly too. This will bring out the animal in you, Peter. You will roar like a boar for more until you are sore."

When I had cleaned the dish to Tora's satisfaction she wiped my mouth and brought in the next course. It looked really appetizing. "Here is famous recipe from my own Norway, Peter," she explained excitedly. "This is fiskeboller med skarp saus; fish balls."

"I didn't realize they had any. . . ."

"This balls is curry hot, darling, which I am serving with asparagus to remind you of me. Very strong potion for lovers. You will want to tear off my peignoir and—how you say in English?—rubbish me."

"Haven't you got any old-fashioned normal food that will calm me, Tora?"

"This is your so lucky night, Peter, because next I have prepared for you a special dish I learned in Sweden. It is called Janssons frestelse but this one I am calling Peter's frestelse, with anchovies, potato, onions, butter and cream. Anchovies are most aphrodisiac, so that you will feel like the bull which is foaming at the mouth."

"May I know what my frestelse is when it's at home, Tora?"

"The name of the dish is Peter's temptation—such that he cannot resist me. With so much rich fish in him he will become—how you say in English?—Jack the Kipper."

It was surprising how such a slim leggy blonde could pack away so much feed. I had no trouble myself because not only was it delicious but also the sauna had sharpened my appetite in all directions. Tora produced wine to wash down the delicacies, yet despite the sauna shirt and squatting on the carpet I kept my British aplomb as though I was banqueting in white tie and tails.

"Lastly for dessert I give you from my own Norway the riskrem, Peter. You call this rice-pud over here but we are using almonds, butter and cream."

"Which will undoubtedly make me scream with lust?"

"Exactly. You English men are so stolid, so correct, so calm that it is necessary to stir you into romantic mood. Otherwise your women will go mad with neglect. You think a woman's purpose in life is to make possible the mixed doubles in tennis, and they are handy for dancing because men find it difficult to go backwards. You will find this hard to believe, Peter, but we are women—*women*!"

I dropped the riskrem in panic as Tora burst out of the peignoir in emphasizing the statement. It was like waking up in bed and suddenly being confronted by the Venus de Milo in the room.

"I too am a *woman*," Tora continued, as if I had just landed from Mars and couldn't tell the difference. "As a man do you know what I need more than anything in the world right now, Peter?"

"A safety-pin?"

"I need my big strong lustful lover."

"You can phone Norway direct now, Tora."

"But he is here, Peter—here in Cudford!"

"Then I'd better beat it fast. If he finds me sitting here in a sauna shirt he'll. . . ."

Tora play-smacked my face impatiently. "But it is you, Peter, you!"

"Me!"

"Oh you English men, so modest, so strong, so silent, so imperturbable—so imbecile. You drive your women crazy with desire but then you need a road map."

"Am I really so attractive, Tora?"

"Magnetic. I worship the lovely earthy ancient smell of your body. You remind me of furniture polish, linseed-oil and turps. Sometimes you are mouldy or beeswaxy or gluey—but always you remind me of wood. Old seasoned English oak."

"Good thing I'm not a pig-keeper then," I observed coldly. This was the first time I became aware that I possessed an occupational smell, which knowledge did not bolster my confidence for future social gatherings. I imagined girls whispering, "Dance with that tall fellow over there and tell me whether you think he's an antique dealer or an undertaker." Then her friend would return to report, "He's not got hot enough yet, Sandra, but probably a carpenter."

"You would turn me on even if you worked in a sewer, darling. Nature fashioned you like a huge phallus with feet. That is why I want you tonight."

Anxiously I checked Apollo's clock for the time but to my consternation it still registered just after nine. I made to fetch my own watch from the bathroom but for some inexplicable reason my legs refused to function. Tora kindly brought it for me and I was surprised that it too registered just after nine.

"Time stands still for lovers, darling," Tora laughed. "See how Apollo is looking at his clock in surprise because it does not move. The night is young and you're so primitive, Peter. Let me help you to the bean-bag settee."

"I can't eat any more, Tora, I'm full to bursting."

"Lie on it, my Viking, not eat it. Remember, we have not a care in the world."

"Speak for yourself, Tora—I have to face Olga."

"Have some more saki and you will forget everything."

"I've already forgotten how to stand up. Must be physical amnesia of the legs."

I did my best to look blasé on the bean-bag settee, which is difficult when one feels like a bag of beans lying on a larger bag of beans. Despite my iron will I have never been a dyed-in-the-wool misogynist—in fact I couldn't even spell it—but on the other hand nor have I been a woman's plaything. Tonight I sensed instinctively that the pendulum was swinging from one extreme to the other so that if my emotional steel bent any further Tora might win the battle for my favours. I might smell of wood but I was certainly not made of it, and there were limits to what even an iron man like myself could endure.

Tora sat beside her heap of Viking exuding Estée Lauder perfume which made me feel I had collapsed at the Chelsea Flower Show. Extremely embarrassing when a beautiful girl

74

insists you are her strong Viking warrior—she had even placed the traditional horned helmet on my head—when in actual fact you have had to ask her to find your head and sort it out of the heap for crowning. Tora's remedy for all ills was more saki, assuring me how this would arouse me in readiness for battle.

"Who do I have to fight, Tora?" I inquired, in case there was competition lurking in the background. Anything fiercer than a mouse would have me at a serious disadvantage.

"I'll give you one guess, my bold warrior. I am only a poor defenceless woman but I shall resist with all my strength— though eventually you will overcome me because I cannot deny you for long. I shall be forced to surrender, darling, for you are like one of the mighty Nordic gods—nobody can stand up to you."

I figured if that was true it would be solely because I couldn't stand up either. We should have to battle to the death lying flat in two heaps.

Tora dimmed the lights and whispered, "Darling, will you do something very personal for me?"

"Sure honey, provided I can do it without moving."

"Will you model for me as Odin, the mighty god of battle?"

"Yes of course, so long as I can pose here on my back with my eyes shut."

"But you are our ancient god of war, Peter."

"Then call it 'Killed in Action'."

"Ah, you naughty one, you are thinking of me."

"Actually, Tora, I was thinking of me."

Tora sighed deeply. "You must understand how I want you to model for me so I may sculpt you in the nude, Peter."

"Won't you find it cold?"

"No, it is you who may find it cold for you will be wearing only the great helmet of bull's horns and holding your spear. Then I can add you to the display shelf alongside all those other lovely men."

Mustering all my reserve strength I sniggered with it. "That is completely out of the question right now because I am rather tired and weak. So weak that this helmet of yours is pinning me to the ground and the wrist-watch could well break my arm."

"I understand, Peter; a man's desire often weakens him so. But you must model for me another time because tonight is reserved for love. Shall we say this night next week?"

"My dear girl, as much as I should like to Olga would never let . . . of course I will, Tora! I will, promise you faithfully! Any time you want, I swear it! HELP! . . . MERCY! . . . SURRENDER! . . ."

Had it come to this in the battle of the sexes that a mere girl was able to change my mind so easily—using only her lighted cigarette?

6

Olga was most understanding and sympathetic about Operation Sexy Pants, as she called it. She dusted the shop more thoroughly than usual, adjusting mirrors and paintings to a tolerance of one thou. of an inch.

"Of course you're tired, Peter, delivering goods after hours. Very exhausting work indeed," she consoled me kindly.

The weary red slits which had formerly been my eyes regarded Olga indirectly via a reproduction Chippendale cheval-glass mirror. I said little because of the hallucination that Olga was enlarging and shrinking every time I moved my huge head, and before I could go through a door I had to wait until it was in the correct position, not oscillating. When I arrived at two or more doors in any one wall it was necessary for me to ascertain by touch which was the door that led through to the other side. This saved me the embarrassment of walking into the wall on each occasion I hurried to the toilet to be desperately ill.

I had not yet recovered from the shock of bending down to tie my shoe-laces, when I had turned a complete somersault in the hall and blacked out. How could you tell Olga that tying laces brought one nigh to death? So I tucked them in my shoes.

My memory had almost deserted me. Olga had to tell me her name seven times before we opened for business, besides showing me where I kept my stock-book. Worse still, I could perform no repairs in the workshop because the furniture seemed to come alive and poke me about the face. Probably few other men have received a black eye from an angry Adam chair leg.

"You acted quite correctly last night," Olga advised me, "because our aim is to satisfy the customer. So you've obviously done that."

"Yes, Olga our customer is to aim the satisfy," I agreed.

"And one night is not long to make such a delivery, Peter. If it had been a bulky article like a sideboard it takes even longer. About a week in your case."

"I'm not well, Olga."

"I did suspect you were slightly off-colour. You may be the first antique dealer to lay down his life for the trade. They'll keep a light ever burning for you at the annual trade fair— to the Unknown Viking Warrior."

"I'm really ill, Olga. I think my brain's damaged."

"Not your brain, Peter. Lower down. Don't see the doctor about it—consult a vet. Cheer up though, lunch will set you right again—old fashioned British belly of pork with pig's liver."

"Ugh!"

Another irritating habit of Olga's was to polish the stock, occasionally emitting a loud exclamation of "Pooh!"

"Scent," she explained when I inquired the reason. "The place reeks as though it's turned back into a barber's shop."

She repeated the observation particularly when I was passing her, emphasizing the pooh by holding her nose and opening windows. I walked gingerly away hoping my enormous head would squeeze through the door without concussing me, but unfortunately I had selected the wrong door out of three and stepped into the wall.

There was a series of five headaches in various areas of my gigantic skull which were gradually linking up, partly caused by the thunder of Olga's bracelets as she gesticulated. What I really dreaded was our shop bell pinging when a client entered. This fear so obsessed me that I tried to muffle the clapper, yet this proved impossible because standing on a chair induced acute mountaineers' vertigo that sent me reeling into the street.

Every hour or so I became so drunk that I must sit bolt upright in a wing armchair to stop the shop revolving, Olga with it.

"Pooh!" Olga gasped. "Smells like someone has smashed a whisky bottle in a beauty-parlour. No wonder your nose matches your eyes, Peter, even without the lipstick."

"You're probably drinking that I've been thinking, Olga," I protested.

"Roughly yes. Plus the other six deadly sins."

For once I was glad to see Lennie Labentrekker come in the shop, despite the bell going off like a firework in my ear. Lennie exported to America and Canada, buying on the principle of famine relief. He possessed an uncanny gift of estimating exactly what you had paid for an article, then offering you a price that allowed you a five percent loss. He was not so much a dealer to us, according to Olga, as a friendly burglar.

"Is Peter dead?" Lennie asked in his blunt way. "If so I'll buy him for export."

"He's in a coma, Lennie, passing slowly away in his sleep. He's been working too hard delivering the goods all night and

satisfying customers. Says he's off to Valhalla where all brave
dealers go who have given their all in the battle of the sexes."

"Well, good thing I popped in, Olga. I always bring you
luck."

"Last time you came you brought me gastric flu."

Lennie used a vocabulary of his own which we had learned
to understand but which gave him a distinct advantage in
bargaining. For instance, when he offered a Queen it meant
£1; two-n-arf was £2 10s.; arf-o'-ten was £5; a Froggie was
£10; a score was £20; a bullseye was £50; £100 was a Chiltern
and so on. He referred to all articles of furniture as bundles or
bundles of firewood, which was not encouraging to the seller.

"I'll give you a score for that old bundle there and take it
off your hands," Lennie offered.

Olga smiled without looking. "I'll run into the kitchen and
put the coffee on for us, Lennie; then while I'm outside you
can steal it and sneak off."

The old bundle in question was a William the Fourth
mahogany wine-cooler on lion's paw feet we had obtained
for £25.

"You certainly know how to hurt a man," Lennie moaned.
"I've got to live as well, you know."

"I'd get a fairer deal from a shoplifter."

"Only trying to tempt you, Olga."

"You'd do better with an apple."

"But we're all brothers in our game trying to help each
other, love."

"Don't drag sex into this, Lennie."

"I gotta make a crust somehow, darling."

"Folks with a new Jag standing outside shouldn't say that.
You need a barrow when you're acting."

Lennie glanced through the window at the Jag and sniggered. "That's the triumph of HP over poverty, Olga. The terms are so extended they've had to write them into my will. To think I shall never live to own it outright."

"I bet you say that to all the millionaires."

"You're young and beautiful, sweetheart, so tell you what I do for you. I'll clear the bundle for a turkey."

A turkey was £25, exactly what we had paid for the wine-cooler. Olga handed Lennie our collecting-tin for the PDSA. "Take it, Lennie. You need it more than the animals. They're merely ill."

"OK, honey, forget it. We all buy too dear at times; I've done it myself in the past.'

"When you bought your first rattle as a baby."

Lennie searched elsewhere in the shop with his little eyes. "Nice bundle there, Olga. How much to an old friend of the family? Break it to me gently."

"To an old friend of the family £50, Lennie, but to you £55."

"She tells me jokes at a time like this with prices on the floor in a dying trade! You want to retire young or something?"

We knew Lennie well enough to know that he was examining the George the Third corner cupboard in figured mahogany with a glass-panelled door while he thought about the wine-cooler. Eventually he would purchase them both when the necessary haggling had been completed to his satisfaction. But it was a case of Greek meets Greek, for Olga possessed limitless patience and would never be persuaded or flattered to accept less than the figure printed in her mind. Sometimes Lennie would return next day—or even next week

—to bargain over a piece, whereas I liked immediate decisions, yes or no. Again, I was satisfied with a quick small profit on a deal but Olga preferred not to sell if a dealer was not prepared to pay almost as much as our retail price.

"Take a trembler on the wine-cooler, Olga," Lennie said suddenly as he sipped our coffee.

"No, Lennie, I'm not giving it away for £30. £40 or nothing, rock bottom."

"Forty thieves! You must be crazy."

The state of play now was that we had obtained the wine-cooler for £25, added a fifty per cent mark up, £37 10s., and Olga was offering it to Lennie for £40. So she was willing to let the trade have it for £35 plus.

"Tell you what I do for you, Olga. Throw in both bundles for a bible."

"Is a bible £80?"

"Three score and ten, £70."

"Can't work out sums like you can, Lennie. Let's do the wine cooler separately. Make me an offer between £40 and forty guineas."

"I never swear in front of a lady, my lover. Give you thirty-five sheets wet with tears."

"Sold."

"So now you've cleaned me out I can't afford the corner cupboard no more, sweetheart."

"I'll cry on your shoulder while you think where you can raise £50. Sell your dear little white haired old mother."

Lennie laughed and put his arm round Olga's waist. "You're the sharpest skirt in the business, lover. You never ought to be beautiful. You should be an ugly hunchback with mittens. Take forty thieves and go to bed laughing that you done a poor old man out of his dinner."

"Make it forty-five and I'll give your a dinner."

"Sold, love, but you may not see me again. Obviously time I retired when a young tart like you takes me pants off at me own game."

Lennie stayed to lunch as usual, then bought some more stock. He licked a label and stuck it on every item purchased before paying us from a rounded wad of fivers as big as a toilet roll.

"Tax avoidance, friends, not tax evasion—that would be illegal and naughty," he smirked every time he did it.

A week later Pickfords would arrive to bind and crate the goods for shipment overseas. Most dealers, however, preferred to shift stock themselves, usually on roofracks or in vans.

The excitement began soon after six that same day with a phone call from the Mellon Auction Galleries. To my surprise Mr Mellon himself was on the other end so I knew it must be important. Normally Mr Mellon handled calls himself only if you owed him money. He wanted to talk about money this time, but in connection with the painting.

"We managed to sell *The Milkmaids*, Pook," he boomed into my ear. "Fetched a very fair price for a Constable."

"A policeman bought it?" I inquired.

"Constable painted it circa 1810, so it created quite a stir."

"It reached reserve price all right then, Mr Mellon?"

"Rather better than reserve because Schinberger, Luffendorp and Swartzstein were all bidding, which pushed up the price a trifle."

"Never heard of them."

"Eventually Schinberger dropped out at one hundred."

"One hundred pounds!"

"One hundred thousand. Then Luffendorp ran Swartzstein up to one-o-five."

"How much is that in money, Mr Mellon. I'm slightly confused."

"Swartzstein of Bond Street bought the painting for one hundred and five thousand pounds, Pook. Six figures. Your reserve was well below that; fifteen pounds if my memory serves me correctly."

I shook my head in an effort to think straight. "Please don't joke, Mr Mellon. I'm already a wreck today."

"I never jest, Pook, as you well know in the sale-room. Take the cheque to the bank and observe if they laugh. However, allow me to congratulate you on your personal gain and your service to Art by rediscovering a lost masterpiece. Good-day to you, sir."

Breaking the news to Olga was even more difficult than Mr Mellon breaking it to me. She accused me of being drunk again, refusing to accept my oath on the Bible until she had rung Mr Mellon herself. Then she forgave me everything.

We hugged and danced round the shop in a fever of excitement, singing and shouting until Olga burst into tears when she discovered I was sobbing into a duster. It was every dealer's dream come true, to happen upon an old master then sell it for a fortune. After so much celebration I lay full-length on a Regency chaise-longue in the window for all the world to see, partly intoxicated from the previous night, partly exhausted by this new sensation. As one in a trance I kept repeating the magic words "One hundred and five thousand pounds!" like some ritual incantation.

"Minus Mr Mellon's commission, Peter," Olga reminded me in her practical way.

You cannot hush up that kind of money by putting an X on the coupon to eliminate publicity. The press seized on the story so quickly that the Cudford Echo was interviewing us that same evening. After I had told reporter Curly Brown that we were giving all the money to charity and that charity begins at home, Olga took over the interviewing.

Abhorring publicity as I did, I thought some small gesture was required to meet the national press who beseiged us next day. So I donned my lettuce-green Caribbean suit which glowed in the dark, teamed with my blaze red-and-yellow tie I had worn to the Derby. A gold floral shirt and black-and-white shoes completed the ensemble except that I could not resist airing my new chequerboard waistcoat with the copper buttons. At the last minute I threw aside my customary conservatism in dress by the daring addition of tartan socks with matching handkerchief. As I left the bedroom I shyly inserted my best pearl tie-clip together with the gold-rope key-chain, then hung my silver anchor-cable watch-chain across the waistcoat.

Praying the reporters would not notice me I stood beside Olga in the shop while she told them the story of our good fortune over and over again. Once the reporters had got the full story—and nobody could make a story fuller than Olga—they plied us with a variety of odd questions connected with Art. Such as was I colour-blind and what did Olga think of men's clothing.

I ventured to tell one reporter, who donned sun-glasses as he listened, that I trusted he would respect my privacy by not pestering me for my life story because I dreaded my remarkable adventures in the Far East being exploited to boost the circulation of the sensational press. He promised me that he would not stoop so low and explained how the press was much more responsible nowadays, then walked away. Sensing a trap I approached another reporter to warn him that I was no easy dupe for any sharp newsman searching for a scoop, no matter how much money he might try to tempt me with. He too commended my caution and hurried off. Further to protect myself from the reporters clustered round Olga I buttonholed each one in turn, giving him fair warning that I refused to be made a victim of Fleet Street journalism by allowing my story to create a nine days wonder so that readers could gloat over the fifteen lurid photographs I displayed to him. There are some things so sordid that a man wants to forget them if he can, I warned him, not prostitute himself further by selling his soul to the Devil for mere gold. Nothing would persuade me to part with the copyright, even to a man like himself who worked for the wealthiest tabloid of them all. The reporter thoroughly agreed with my high ideals, advising me to ensure my future peace of mind by burning them.

When the flash-bulbs began to pop I hurried to Olga's side to protect her from unhealthy exposure but she did not seem to want it. In fact the photographers produced technical reasons why better results could be obtained if I stood apart from Olga, such as behind the cameras. One bearded expert, hung with cameras like an equipment rack, went so far as to suggest that I should pose for him in the workshop. I went out there and posed but he failed to turn up. Meanwhile Olga was photographed in a variety of positions; polishing a Victorian rosewood card table on bun feet with her bust out; laughing gaily as she dusted the very top of a late seven-teenth century oak buffet, fully stretched to show plenty of nylon thigh; holding a George the Third silver coffee pot in rapturous admiration; sitting on a low William the Fourth walnut couch with cabriole legs to display her own long legs to just under one metre.

I heard one reporter laugh, "What a break! A hot story *and* a beautiful bird!"

"Who's the cuckoo with her wearing the Union Jack out-fit?" inquired a photographer.

"That's her partner, bud. Must think he's a colour-chart."

Unobtrusively I carried my work bench into the shop, then began to rub down a Queen Anne chair-leg, at the same time singing a traditional cabinetmaker's rubbing down ditty to portray a true craftsman loving his work.

"Do hope the noise of this ancient craftsmanship doesn't disturb you fellows," I called out to the group about Olga's legs but nobody turned round. "No doubt you're all wonder-ing how we restore our priceless heritage from the past, so here you can actually see it being done."

Someone muttered, "If you don't shut up you'll get done," so I switched on the electric drill with sandpaper attachment.

"Of course in this day and age we speed up the process with the aid of modern technology but we still maintain the high precision standards of Chippendale and his illustrious peers. . . ."

Embarrassed, I stopped shouting and switched off the sander because I was no longer holding a Queen Anne chair-leg so much as a Queen Anne walking-stick. The efficiency of modern technology appalled me as I regarded the pile of saw-dust that had once been a chair-leg, leaving me with a kind of mahogany meat-skewer with a castor on one end. How could you sell a three-legged Queen Anne chair? It could not even be passed off as a luxurious milking-stool used by Queen Anne at a court masque.

Then suddenly I remembered it did not matter any more. With a fortune in the bank we could afford tiny errors of judgement on my part; like the day the drill was delivered to us. Its first job was to make a peg-hole to reinforce one end of an Edwardian mahogany bed with painted panels. Accustomed to my father's original brace-and-bit I exerted too much pressure, and in seconds the drill had pierced right through the faulty panel-support, and in addition the bed was now secured to the wall by the steel bit.

As for the circular-saw attachment, Olga had forbidden its use on the grounds that I would end up selling firewood with no fingers. I possessed a flair for depriving tables of their legs when repairing them, but my secret shame was accidentally sawing my sawing tressle in half, simultaneously sustaining a damaged shoulder where I hit the floor of the workshop as a result. Olga was aware only of the accidents she witnessed, so I did not bother her with minor slips such as the reamer which I was still endeavouring to dig out of my work-bench, or the circular rasp file buried in the ceiling like a musket-ball.

Confidentially, my damaged shoulder and three bandaged fingers did not enhance the feeling that I was a master craftsman like Adam and Hepplewhite, no matter how I tried. It was difficult to convince myself that Thomas Sheraton's workshop was littered with off-cuts of tables and halves of chair-legs and three-legged sofas, nor were his table-tops punctured by holes bored too deep from below. Surely Mrs Sheraton never handed him a damaged footstool, telling him to get busy and wreck it.

The Victorian tract hanging over my work-bench reminded us that 'A Bad Workman Always Blames His Tools'. Olga had placed it there some time ago before the introduction of the electric drill when I excused my faults because I lacked modern equipment. Nor would she accept my plea that the only obstacle between me and success was my being left-handed, when everybody knows how tools are designed for right-handed craftsmen. She was quick to point out that Leonardo da Vinci was left-handed and as far as she could ascertain he had to struggle on with his work without a Black & Decker multi-purpose drill. However, as I persisted in my argument she offered to buy me a left-handed hammer, chisel and screwdriver for Christmas provided I showed her where they were to be obtained.

One of the great mysteries of my career was my inability to become a master craftsman like Inigo Jones or Grinling Gibbons. I did all the things they did. I loved wood, felt its texture and patina, even smelt it, yet directly I applied tools to it the cursed stuff split, cracked, splintered, attacked me and often turned red with blood. Its edges grew curved under my plane, zigzag under my saw and downright ragged under my chisel. Sometimes not only did I break the wood but also the wood broke my tools in a kind of revenge. I have never revealed this before, but often when Olga was out shopping and screws were snapping off deep in the woodwork, nails were folding up under the hammer and timber was splitting under the chisel, I would bandage my fingers, seize a mallet and unashamedly attack the furniture with it as I shouted the terrible oaths the craft had taught me. I could not imagine William

Kent emerging from his workshop enraged, big-veined and trembling, to roar that he had managed to slaughter an obstinate commode.

But there were successes too. If I learned nothing else in the trade I learned to stop my work wobbling. My favourite item was the three-legged stool because it cannot wobble. Anything on four or six legs I steadied by fixing various sized caps under the short legs, although tiny wobbles responded to drawing-pins. My original method of sawing off the bottom of five legs to match the sixth taught me this after I had gradually reduced a dining-table to an enormous coffee-table, so low that the folding leaves rested on the carpet. Olga suggested we sell it to an Indian family who would be prepared to squat round it on the floor.

Because the right-angled joint was beyond the capabilities of my saw I learned to fill in the gap with plastic wood. Another boon was my discovery that the surplus ripples of cloth left after re-covering a chair seat could be eliminated by soaking it with hot water. When the material dried it was stretched satisfyingly tight by shrinkage.

When at last the reporters and photographers departed to refresh themselves in the Flying Bull and Olga and I were left in peace to think about tidying up the debris of the mass media we heard a voice calling us. The shrill insistent voice we knew so well.

"Greeting from your lord and master, humble artisans! Cancel the bow and curtsey lest they delay the wine. Let us celebrate, for that which was lost has been found!"

Into the shop clumped the small aggressive figure of the Honourable Lesley Pilkington-Goldberg, his retroussé nose red with joy, his face one vast smirk. "I come down from the exclusive realm of the aristocracy to visit the common people who engage in trade. But enough of sensation, restrain your awe, wipe those tears of bliss, rise from your knees—then uncork a bottle fast."

Honners had arrived in force.

7

"No-one is perfect," Honners laughed, holding Olga's hand and ogling at her. "Even I am not entirely immune to my tipple."

"You're not immune to our tipple either," I observed, as he kept refilling his glass without being asked. Another of Honners' faults he didn't know about was this habit of speaking to you as though you were a meeting. Even on the phone he seemed to believe he was a general addressing an army on the eve of battle. If Honners met you on Waterloo Station many travellers thought he was the public-address system.

"Do I really?" he had once replied when I questioned him about it. "Never mind, Peter, most people are mentally deaf anyway so I believe in getting through their thick skulls to the vacuum inside. That's why I have to shout at you. I am Nature's answer to television."

Olga was obviously flattered by Honners' attention so she did not withdraw her hand. In fact she gave him the other one. "You must have heard about our good fortune, Honners," she cooed.

"Your good fortune, my lovely, is receiving me in your little house. But as I spread my largesse in lavish dollops I assume you refer also to the Constable canvas."

"Yes of course."

Honners lit a fresh cigar and puffed till the three of us sat there in localized fog. "I descend from the lofty portals of the blood royal to come among you as though I were but an ordinary man in order to congratulate you, Olga. Peter has rendered to my family in the past so many outstanding disservices that I am loath to believe he is connected with the rediscovery of Constable's *Milkmaids*—or, as we call it up at The Hall, *The Country Bouncers*."

"Please don't be vulgar, Honners," Olga smiled indulgently.

"A contradiction of terms, me love, like telling me not to be poor. Vulgarity comes only from the vulgar, but that is above your pretty head. My visit tonight is to thank you and to inform you that I am already in touch with Swartzstein of Bond Street for the restoration of the oil-painting."

"Most old pictures need restoring, Honners, but may I ask why it concerns you?"

Honners laughed shrilly as he refilled his glass. "Well spoken, nubile wench. Most old pictures, as you insist upon calling great masterpieces, do need restoring but this one needs a special kind of restoring—restoring to me."

"To you!"

"Indeed. *The Milkmaids* was stolen from the Long Gallery up at The Hall some years ago, hence my visit here to express my indebtedness to you for accomplishing what the police failed to do. Let us open another bottle of wine in celebration, for that which was lost has been found."

"But Peter bought that painting, Honners," Olga protested.

"Naturally. One does not suppose that he knocked it off. May one inquire how much he paid for it?"

"Well, if you must know, nine pounds."

"Nine pounds! Quite a bargain even for Peter, our latter-day Shylock. Slightly more profit than your normal fifty per cent mark up, eh? Let me see; one hundred and five thousand pounds less Mellon's commission at ten per cent, that leaves —the old brain isn't as quick as it used to be—that leaves ninety-four thousand and five hundred pounds. Nice work, Olga."

"That's what we thought, Honners."

"Unfortunately, darling, there is the question of the LAW. Now the LAW insists that one cannot possess goods without a TITLE to them, nor can one obtain a TITLE for goods from a party who himself possesses no TITLE, even for monies paid to that party in good faith. To illustrate, if I purchase a car from a party who stole that car I have no TITLE in LAW. My sole redress is against the thief—if I can find him—and the car reverts to the party from whom the car was stolen, for he owns the TITLE in LAW."

"I do follow your argument, Honners. Please don't emphasize everything as though I am a convention where you are selling deaf-aids."

"Merely my endeavours to demonstrate how the painting is still mine, Olga."

"But Peter paid for it, Mr Mellon auctioned it, and Swartzstein have given their cheque to Mr Mellon. He deducted his commission and made out his cheque to Peter."

Honners threw his arms wide. "All in vain, Olga. Peter didn't realize it, Mellon didn't realize it, Swartzstein didn't realize it—but no TITLE in LAW. They were selling what was not theirs to sell. Just as if I sold you Buckingham Palace for a million quid your chances of moving in downstairs and letting the top flat would be pretty slim."

"You mean we've been done!" I gasped.

"As usual, Peter, your acute brain has grasped the situation in a flash. A remarkably slow flash but grasped it all the same. However, laddie, do not despair, for the reward my family offered originally still stands."

"Knowing your family, Honners, means that I'll stand to receive as much as a fiver."

"On the contrary. Our high reputation of preserving our cultural heritage for the nation is such that my pater offered five per cent of the then estimated value. For tax purposes he put it at five thousand pounds."

"So at least I'll get five thousand pounds, Honners."

"Not quite. Five per cent is two hundred and fifty pounds."

"Can I claim bus fare too?" I asked disgustedly.

"Ah, we must be guided by our solicitors on that point."

"Do I pay them as well?"

"Oh, Peter, it's all in the luck of the game. Learn to take the rough with the smooth. Now let us eat, drink, and be merry for tomorrow we get *The Country Bouncers* bouncing back on our wall in the Long Gallery."

The police often dropped in our shop with lists of stolen property but next day Constable Barrington drove up on his panda bicycle, then limped into the shop on a different mission. Constable Barrington had known me well since my childhood, when he had often predicted I would hang directly they released me from Dartmoor. He worked on the theory that you were guilty until proved innocent by clever lying. Then he got you for perjury.

Charges I recall were no light on my fairy-cycle; three passengers on one bicycle; assisting the apple harvest at midnight; fishing in Cudford Ornamental Lake; kissing Hilda Longbothem on Lord Kirkdale's Tomb; Guinness bottle label in my first car's tax disc; wooing Betty Pillock inside the marble statue of the Trojan Horse at Cudford Park.

Constable Barrington was the original one-man Scotland Yard. "Tell you my weaknesses what deprived me of promotion," he informed me every time I was caught. "I'm just a simple old village flatfoot, yet I got a streak of unnatural cunning, Pook. I'm cruel too, almost sadistic you might say, never giving up the chase not if it takes me twenty years to find the yob what done it—though in your case twenty minutes. Another fault of mine is being able to detect a liar, 'cos when you lies it's like a big neon sign lights up on top of your head similar to these new-fangled petrol-pumps, with LIAR all wrote in bright red tubin'. Another of my weaknesses is being strong and eighteen stone and six-foot-three, 'cos this makes me a right old bully and leads to police brutality when I'm arrestin' five or six thugs what done an old lady over. And when they says it was her fault because she was carrying a purse with her pension in, which amounts to deliberate provocation on her part and she ought to be punished for making them attack her I laughs summink cruel—enough to hurt their subconscious social inhibitions so bad that even the Welfare State psychiatrists can't do nothing with them except learn them the guitar. Oh yes, Pook, my life's been a miserable failure, yet somehow I keeps the peace on my manor summink cruel."

Constable Barrington relentlessly clumped into the shop and filled it up. "Mornin' Olga and partner. I always says a life of petty crime leads to the big stuff. Come in to ask Pook to save time and reduce his sentence by telling me all about knocking Honners' picture off, hiding it a few years, then selling it for a fortune."

"I bought it legitimately, Constable Barrington," I said

simply. "If you heard a man was murdered in Australia you'd call in here and ask me why I quarrelled with him last night."

"That's what they all plead, Pook, Let's have it from the beginning how you done it while I write it down in evidence against you. Number one, how much did you allegedly pay for the picture."

"Nine pounds."

"Ho-hum, nine . . . pounds," Constable Barrington laboriously recorded in the notebook I knew so well. "Can't be dear, eh? Who sold you this priceless old master for nine pounds —Father Christmas?"

"A Mrs Kendal."

"Oh, Mother Goose, eh? Where does she live?—and don't tell me in a Crooked House."

"Number 3, Meadow Rise, Cudford."

"Ah-ha. What was her occupation—art dealer?"

"As far as I could gather she was a fortune-teller."

"I bet she was! Did you get a receipt so your tax returns would be accurate, Pook?"

"Of course. Here it is."

Constable Barrington removed his helmet and scratched his head to let me see he was puzzled, even amazed. "A Mrs X! Ho-ho-ho-ho—a Mrs X, Pook!"

"The old lady couldn't read or write. That's her mark."

"Didn't think it was a kiss, but when a party signs with a mark there's got to be witnesses to that mark."

"We were alone. I was the only witness."

"No, Pook, you're an interested party. Witnesses have to be disinterested. Where were you on the night of Monday, 2nd April, 1945?"

"Good grief, Constable, in bed I expect. Can't recall who

with. You can't suddenly name a date years ago, then ask me what I was doing. It's ridiculous. Who could possibly remember? Let me try it on you. What were you doing that night?"

"It was Easter Monday and I was off duty so I takes me missus to see *The Pirates of Penzance* by Cudford Operatic Society at seven-thirty, then we had a jug in the Bold Forester afore they closed. Three-and-a-tanner each the seats was, and next to us was Gus Piper and his missus as witnesses as you might say. You weren't there so where was you?"

"How do you know all that?"

"Always keeps a diary, of course. Now where was you?"

"How do I know?"

"Then I'll tell you where you was. You was home from the Far East on LEAP leave for one month and Monday night Honners invited you up The Hall for supper."

"How could you possibly know all that?"

"Honners always keeps a house journal."

"But what has this got to do with the painting?"

"That's the night it was nicked. Circumstantial evidence is very strong, Pook—as the man said when he found a salmon in the milk. You're feeding your face till Honners kicks you out at midnight. Theft discovered next morning. Funny."

"Well, the obvious thing is to question Mrs Kendal, not me."

"Good thinking, Pook. We questions everybody until we get right back to you. No time like the present, as the defendant said when the judge had a heart-attack."

I drove Constable Barrington out to Meadow Rise in the brake, confident my name would be cleared. I pulled up at

98

number 3 with a strange feeling in my bones because the colour of the trailer had changed from white to blue. Even worse it had got bigger. Worst of all the lady who opened the door had changed to brown, obviously a Pakistani. She greeted me effusively but after the preliminary exchange of courtesies I gathered that though she spoke English she did not understand it.

"Excuse me, madam, but do you know Mrs Kendal?" I inquired.

"Oh yes indeed," she replied, laughing every time she spoke.

"Does she still live here?"

"Oh yes indeed."

"May I speak to her, please?"

"Oh yes indeed."

This produced no action because the lady stood regarding me with a broad smile. I tried again on a different tack.

"Has Mrs Kendal left here, madam?"

"Oh yes indeed."

"When did she move house?"

"Oh yes indeed."

Constable Barrington growled impatiently. "Waste of time, Pook. You lived out East so try her own lingo."

"I don't know every Eastern tongue though."

"She's from Pakistan. Surely you knows that one."

"I'll do my best."

I began to address the lady in Pakistani—basic Pakistani I recalled from the past—waving my head and arms as Englishmen do when conversing in a foreign language, on the principle that physical jerks compensate for lack of vocabulary. For her part she laughed inordinately, as foreigners do in order not to appear rude and offend an idiot.

"Oh yes indeed!" she roared, waggling her own head delightedly as if I were a door-to-door juggler who had called to entertain her.

"You in't exactly got the gift of tongues, have you, Pook?" Constable Barrington needled me. "If you was an interpreter at the United Nations there'd never be no more war—they wouldn't know how to declare it."

"Can you communicate any better then?"

"Couldn't do no worse unless I was dead. Watch."

With his usual direct approach Constable Barrington bowed to the lady, smiled and removed his helmet, whereupon she automatically extended an arm for us to enter. Deceptively agile for his bulk Barrington glided inside and cased the trailer in seconds. "Your Mrs Kendal don't live here and never did, Pook," he barked. "Let's try next door."

Of the three trailers that constituted Meadow Rise number 1 was empty and number 2 housed the wife of a farm worker who "Didn't know nothing, didn't see nothing and didn't mix with nobody." Her sole contact with the outside world was by television, a one-way process which precluded knowledge of Mrs Kendal because Mrs Kendal did not appear on the screen of her set. On the other hand, had we been searching for Ena Sharples or Hughie Green she would have been a mine of information.

"You in't under arrest yet, Pook," Constable Barrington advised me as we drove home, "but don't choose this particular time for a holiday in South America. Meanwhile I'll report back to me superiors, then check when they wants you flung in jail."

When I explained events to Olga she grimaced. "You are in

a spot of bother," she observed shrewdly.

"You would have said that to Charles the First on the block. How come you took all the credit with the press, yet I have to take the can back when it comes to proving ownership?"

"I didn't buy the blessed painting, Peter—you did. As I remarked to Tora only this morning, you seem to be trouble-prone."

"Tora!"

"Oh, she rushed in panting with desire to remind you about some modelling date. Said she's anxious to do you in cement, wearing a silly helmet over your birthday suit. Said you had a body like a bull so I pointed out that it came with matching brain."

"I can't worry about Tora at a time like this, Olga. Barrington reckons I could get ten years inside."

"What you need right now is an alibi, Peter. Don't tell me you visited The Hall without some girl in tow."

I laughed unsmilingly. "Barrington wouldn't accept that kind of alibi unless she was Queen Victoria. Besides, how can anyone find out that sort of information after so many years?"

"How did Honners remember the details? Think hard."

"He keeps a house journal, Volume 387 or thereabouts, like all the big houses do, similar to a ship's logbook. Everything goes in it—even what you ate and how much. That's why he knows so much history, like King James forbidding anybody to smoke and Henry the Eighth demanding an extra pillow."

"So there's bound to be a guest list in it. Check which floozie was with you, look her up, then she might give you one of those sexy alibis you read about in the papers: 'He stayed with me all that night, says Murder Suspect's Moll'."

"Isn't it marvellous, Olga? I bought an old picture in the normal course of business and now I'm a murder suspect."

"All you need is a firm alibi. Honners' house journal is your best bet. It worked for him so why not for you?"

"Supposing—just supposing—there was a girl that night. Supposing I could even trace her. Do you imagine she would be prepared to give me that sort of alibi? I mean, would you if you were in her position?"

Olga went all prissy. "The question would not have arisen because I'm not that kind of a girl. But some would just for the publicity—or money. They're obviously not going to locate Mrs Kendal so really you've got no choice. If it were me I'd be up The Hall right now trying to build some sort of case for the defence. What else is there?"

We were interrupted by the arrival of Yosseff in search of a Regency rosewood gaming table with splay feet and Olga attached, so I drove over to The Hall while I was urgently not needed.

Honners greeted me as though we were duellists who had accidentally met at the gunsmith's. "Anything within the law to assist an ex-friend clear his name," he said pompously after hearing of my mission. "Never let it be said that a Pilkington-Goldberg put any obstacle in the path of justice. Therefore Exhibit A is at your disposal for a full five minutes."

"But surely you don't think I, of all people, would nick your picture, Honners?" I protested.

"I think nothing, Peter, I am thoughtless, about who nicked my picture—as you please to call the art theft of the century.

That is for the law to decide. I have suffered enough, staring for years at that horrible gap upon the wall of the Long Gallery between Turner and Millais tormented by the nightmare that I may have nursed a viper in my bosom, heartbroken by the cultural loss to the nation, conscience-stricken that I failed the trust of my illustrious forbears, haunted by the recriminations of my descendants, angry that I was hoodwinked by cupidity disguised as friendship. . . ."

"I only want a quick peek at your journal, Honners."

"That you may have, Peter, for old times sake but I shall insist upon being present throughout the peek."

Honners opened the ancient Chubb safe in his study, withdrew a steel document box which required two keys, one from his pocket and one a long way off. I say that because he left me for ten minutes before returning with it. Inside the box lay a kind of leather-bound volume which itself was locked by means of a brass clasp.

"Don't want every Tom, Dick and Harry nosing into the house journal," Honners explained as he unlocked the clasp from his key-chain.

"Tom, Dick and Houdini," I corrected him.

"Jokes in the face of adversity! Such courage. Let me see, Volume 487—my, how time flies—A.D. 1945."

"Don't tell me you've got B.C. ones!"

"No, Peter, we only go back to A.D. 1458 in our house journals. Prior to that the records are in manuscript. Ah, here we are, Monday, 2nd April. Let me see, breakfast so-and-so, mowed the East Lawns, checked the tomatoes in the Glass House, galloped Red Rascal mile and a half, Lady Kirkdale to lunch—her poodle wet the wall-to-wall Wilton—opened Cudford Easter Fête on the North Lawns in the afternoon, profit £357 18s. 9¾d.—record crowd and an excellent take—dealt with my personal correspondence from six to seven. . . ."

"Excuse me, Honners, but if you turn over two pages we'll find the evening story begins."

". . . Seven to seven-thirty completed house journal entries for yesterday, dressed for dinner, wore the black . . . ah, here is the vital information. Guest List . . . Peter Pook wearing a suit obviously purloined from a refugee clothing shipment, escorting Miss Sonia Barrington wearing such a low-cut gown that at table she appeared to be a nude sheltering behind a silver cruet. . . ."

I gasped aloud. "Sonia Barrington! How it all comes back to me!"

Honners sniggered. "As I recall it she had an awful lot to come back. All body and no brain. As though she was one of those milkmaids in the painting and had toppled forward into the room because of her bust weight."

"All woman—and how she worshipped me. Said she suffered from such a strict upbringing that I was her release. We packed a whole married life into about three weeks."

"Then why did you part?"

"To save me from a nervous breakdown. . . ."

"Well, Peter, you've seen the journal, checked its veracity and broken my heart with romantic nostalgia, so now buzz off before our lawyers suspect us of collusion."

"Save me from a nervous breakdown! Honners, I've got it!"

"Then shove off and have it at home on the National Health. Anyone taken ill at The Hall runs the risk of being shot by the vet."

"No, Honners, you don't understand. Sonia's home life

was so terribly strict that she became a kind of nubile nun. That suited me except that courting her was the worst experience I ever had."

"Probably her worst experience too. Like being wooed by two octopuses at once."

"Her dad terrorized me night and day to such an extent that when Sonia and I managed to visit a movie as far away as London we sat there trembling in each other's arms. That's why I brought her up to The Hall, what with your security system plus the moat and drawbridge. It wasn't so much a shotgun wedding I dreaded but a shotgun funeral."

Honners' face lit up. "Yes, now I remember, Peter. You told her I was throwing a fancy-dress party, that was why you arrived as a bearded parson."

"Exactly. Sounds ridiculous, Honners but I wore that beard and glasses disguise every time we met. She began to think I was a missionary until . . . good heavens, until that very night!"

"You stood there clean-shaven and put your eight arms round her?"

I shook my head confusedly, unable to say another word as the whole affair screened in my mind like a newsreel. The frightening courtship, the persecution by Sonia's father, that night of love after Honners' party, the consequences of my youthful folly. I walked from The Hall a broken man, my thoughts gripped in a vice. Over and over again I repeated the same question to myself.

Why of all the girls in my love life—did it have to be Constable Barrington's daughter?

8

Olga was extremely busy upholding an old custom reserved only for clients who were rich Arab princes—a free tea behind the shop. As I corpsed wretchedly over the threshold I heard her telling Yosseff how wicked he was, the naughtiest sheik in the world, and if ever he did it again she would never speak to him as long as she lived.

I peeked through the curtain into the back parlour, as Olga called it, to see her punctuating her remarks by waving the left arm in the air like a belly-dancer. On the wrist was a gold bracelet, from which hung a variety of charms in the shapes of camels, sphinxes, crescent moons and twisted rams' horns—all worked in gold.

Yosseff was smiling broadly despite Olga's tirade. "The ram's horn is our ancient fertility symbol, my beautiful one."

"And here's silly me thinking it was an ice-cream cone!" Olga giggled delightedly. "Is there no end to your naughtiness, you wicked boy! For two pins I would smack you."

"Then you shall have two golden pins surmounted with precious stones, O my moon goddess. Nothing is too good for the beautiful mother of my sons."

I entered the room feeling very much a huge gooseberry with bad news. Olga waved to me with the arm which rang like a small tambourine. "Just look what this terrible man has given me for my birthday, Peter!" she cried.

"Birthday!" Was there no end to the shocks today?

"Yes, I was born, you know. The date is recorded, then when the anniversary comes round each year a lot of folks celebrate it with cards, even gifts. Others prefer the old custom of standing there and gasping the traditional greeting of 'Birthday?'"

"Ah ... I have a present for you as well, Olga."

"Why, have the rates come due?"

"No a nice present you'll like."

"Sounds as though you intend keeping it. What is it?"

"A surprise, Olga."

"The biggest surprise you can give me is a present. Where is it?"

"Ah ... I sent away for it but so far it hasn't arrived."

"Don't trust the post, Peter. We're still waiting for last year's. Takes a long time to get a panda from China."

"Olga, I don't want to interrupt your business tea but could I please see you privately for a second?"

"You've bought me a bra?"

"Urgent!"

My eyes enlarged to such an extent as I said it that Olga accompanied me into the shop and stood by the fire-extinguisher ready for an emergency. "What's happened, Peter?" she asked.

I raised finger to lips for one of those sotto voce conversations essential in any business enterprise. "Seen Honners' house journal. Bad news," I hissed in the telegram language I seemed to employ so often lately.

"The bad news is that you've been smoking again," Olga sniffed, now she knew the shop was not on fire.

"That girl I went with, then we spent the night together—
who on earth do you think she was?"

"Anybody's?"

"Sonia Barrington—Constable Barrington's daughter!"

"How cosy! Goes to show what a small world we live in."

"What do you advise me to do, Olga?"

"Stop shaking, then give me my birthday present before
they put you away."

"Seriously, Olga, you must help me."

Olga went into deep thought pose, then said, "Sonia Barrington married that fellow who was always after me. What
ever was his name? Got it—Jim something . . . Jim Fisher. I'll
look him up in Kelly's Directory. Gosh, Fisher sure is a
popular name. Here we are: 'Fisher, James Philip Montescue'.
What a mouthful! Address is Flat 29, Councillor Evans
Court, Mafeking Road. Now, Peter, pop round there right
away and fix up your alibi."

"And check that it's OK with him I suppose. He'd kill
me."

"If you don't come back we'll know he has. Listen, go now
while he's still out at work. Meet Sonia, butter her up, estab-
lish a rapport, put on the act like you do for me, see how
she feels. She may do it for you—you won't know unless you
try. Hint that if she clears you there could be a share in the
reward. See what I'm driving at?"

"Do you really think I could still qualify for the reward?"

"Of course. Once you prove you didn't steal the picture
then you automatically become the finder."

My face lit up at last. "I go, I go—swift as an arrow from
Cupid's bow."

"Then come back slow—for I have Yosseff in tow," Olga

laughed, ringing the charm-bracelet. "By the way, Peter, I nearly forgot. Tora phoned while you were out. Said she wants you round her place Friday night at sex o'clock."

"Sex o'clock!"

"That's what she said. Chicken supper, too, with plenty of breast and leg for you."

I ran out of the shop rather than hear more of Tora's message in my present circumstances.

They say never go back if you don't want to be disappointed, but in Sonia's case it was different. I wasn't so much disappointed as dismayed. They say also that a good start is half the battle, so I lost that half right away. Sonia was a tall curvaceous blonde with only one defect; she used a gritty face-powder which tended to get in my teeth when we kissed. On the credit side she breathed deeply when talking to you, as though she was standing on a yacht riding at anchor, illustrating that beautiful line 'On the bosom of the ocean'.

The door of Flat 29 was opened by a huge blousy woman wearing a dressing-gown and equipped with the day rig of hair-rollers, cigarette and *Daily Mirror*. "Not today thanks," she said through the cigarette.

I turned on the charm. "Sorry to bother you, madam, but I'm looking for a Mrs Fisher."

"I'm Mrs Fisher."

"So I've got the right address. May I speak to your daughter-in-law, please."

The woman looked puzzled. "I haven't got a daughter, let alone a daughter-in-law."

"Not a Mrs Sonia Fisher, madam?"

"There's only one Sonia Fisher I know of and that's me."

"You! . . . I mean the lady in question was a Miss Sonia Barrington . . . I must have got the addresses wrong. . . ."

"That's me all right—Peter Pook. I remember you well enough, you haven't changed much. I'll give you the code word, my pet name for you—Bucephalus. That should ring a bell."

"Bucephalus! You actually called me a Greek god?"

"No, a Greek horse. Alexander the Great's favourite stallion. You were so passionate—the best man I ever had. Come in and have a cup of tea, or a Worthington if you fancy something stronger."

Bewildered, I found myself physically dragged into the kitchen by this enormous woman who had once tantalized me beyond measure. She thrust me into a chair, turned off the radio, opened a quart of Worthington and lit me a cigarette. "Just like old times, Peter," she sighed, coyly sitting on my lap and crushing me. Then she opened another quart bottle for herself.

I quaffed the beer like an alcoholic to dull my senses. "Here's to those good old days, Sonia," I toasted.

"As you can see I haven't lost my figure, Peter," she pointed out superfluously, breathing heavily for maximum bust movement.

"You certainly have not, Sonia," I gasped, thinking she had added two more to the original. "I don't want to appear unromantic, dear, but you'll have to get off me because I can't breathe properly." This was more a polite euphemism for being flattened in a hydraulic press.

"Suppose I've put on a bit of weight lately, Peter. It's my old trouble just like when we first met."

"Eating too much?"

"Frustration, darling. Remember how strict my dad used to be?"

"He made me a white-haired old man with a nervous tic."

"Then I married Jim—and he had to be a long-distance coach-driver. Oh the endless lonely nights and empty days. No wonder I have a weight problem—cream cakes and chocolates don't make up for a husband."

"But I suppose he's home weekends, Sonia?"

"What! From Istanbul? Then he volunteered to do the overland run to Pakistan so he can be home for Christmas Day and Boxing Day. But don't let's talk about Jim; let's talk about us. Haven't you had a lot of publicity in the papers this week!"

Encouraged by the good news about Sonia's husband I explained my present predicament as delicately as I could, playing up the reward and probing to see if she would supply me with an alibi.

"I shall never forget that wonderful night we spent together, Peter," she confirmed, taking out the pink hair-rollers and removing her glasses. "I expect you remember me just like this."

"No, Sonia, to be honest I don't. You've changed . . . there's so much more of you everywhere."

"That's because I'm a neglected suburban wife, like you read about. Do you know what I want more than anything else in the world, Peter?"

"A strict diet?"

"I need a lover. A big strong man like yourself who will sweep me up in his arms and carry me to the stars—like you used to do, Peter."

"We'd have to take the lift this time, Sonia; I couldn't carry you up the stairs, let alone the stars."

Sonia regarded me so hungrily that for a moment I knew how a doughnut felt, helpless on the cake-doily. "Please, Sonia, will you be my alibi if they send me to the Assizes?" I begged.

Without hesitation she replied, "Of course, Peter love. Justice must be done, so it is my duty to protect the man who loved me. What is worse than a woman who does not stick by her man? I shall go to court and tell the truth and nothing but the truth, no matter what it may cost me personally."

I smiled at last, the long smile of relief and gratitude. "Thanks a million, darling, for saving my life. You don't know what this means to me. How can I ever repay you?"

"Come round again tonight at eight o'clock and I'll show you, lover," Sonia smiled into my eyes.

"What do you mean?"

"Well, darling, your alibi is a big thing for a woman to have to do—even for her lover. So I couldn't possibly do it for anyone who wasn't my lover."

"I was your lover so your conscience is clear, Sonia."

"I am a woman, Peter. I cannot do it for a man who isn't my lover."

I swallowed hard on hearing the change of tense. The last thing I wanted to end up as was a crash slimming diet.

"You know my father was very strict, Peter, and brought me up to be religious. He wanted me to become a nun."

"Really? You would have shut the convent down in a week."

"But actually I was such a sexy girl. I didn't tell my sexy friends I was religious."

"And I don't suppose you told your religious friends you were sexy."

"They soon found out, Peter. See you can't keep your hands off me, can you?"

"Where else can I put them, Sonia?—you seem to be everywhere."

"That's because you are my dream man, darling."

"I am?"

"To me you are a god, strong and masculine."

"You really think I'm so attractive, Sonia?"

"You drive me crazy with your flaunting manhood, Peter."

"I do?"

"What woman could possibly resist you?—tell me that."

"I can give you an alphabetical list of their names."

"Nonsense, Peter, no woman could be immune to your rugged features, beautiful as the rocky coast of Ireland battered by the Atlantic storms, lashed by the ocean's fury."

"Oh!"

"But above all it is your distinctive smell that really turns me on, you monster you!"

"My smell!"

"That fascinating aroma of old wood, Rentokil and Ronuk polish. If I had to sum up your charms in one word I would say musty, ancient, earthy—the unforgettable odour of a deserted auction-room at eventide."

"That's a pretty long word, Sonia."

"You remind me of carpets and bedsteads, but more than anything you are woody—timber and all things associated with it."

"Woodworm?"

"I see you as a kind of huge wardrobe packed with surprises from the past, waiting to be explored. The smell is intoxicating."

"Mothballs!"

I jested merely to hide my chagrin concerning my image with women. Again I asked myself why I could not have a romantic love life like other men; moonlight and roses, rather than having to base my sex-appeal on furniture polish and Flit. My pride hurt, I determined to make a stand.

"Sonia, I am not a wardrobe but a man of honour. No matter what the cost I will not pander to your eccentric tastes."

Sonia smiled, and when she smiled there was a great deal of facial area to pucker up. "No alibi then," she sighed.

"Too bad, Sonia. I'd rather face prison than blackmail."

"Well, when you've gone home and thought it over carefully come back here tonight around eight. Then I'll turn up the sensual-heating system to keep us cosy and you can tell me some more about your high-minded principles. See you, loverboy."

Indignantly I bit my lip where an obstinate Victorian mahogany pot cupboard had deliberately punched me in the mouth during repairs. This, I told myself bitterly, was the ultimate humiliation, the final step in my long considered resolve to break with women completely. If they persisted in treating me like a plaything for their amusement they would now have to face a new type of man, hard as carborundum, cold as ice and tough as the oak I fought in my workshop—until I became known as Impregnable Pook.

I sat in the sale-room at the foot of Mr Mellon's rostrum as though we were in church. I felt pretty bushed and unbelievably old. In fact, Mr Mellon inquired if it was my father come to bid on my behalf. I had never before sat in the sale-room but this morning my legs refused to support me for any length of time. Worse still, when the dizzy spells hit me I didn't know if my legs were supporting me or not.

"Are you ill, Mr Pook?" the auctioneer asked, after six rolls of coconut-matting had been knocked down to me because I had cried out for a chair to sit on.

"I shall be if you push that coconut-matting on my bill, sir," I replied. "I merely wanted a chair."

"The set of chairs do not come up till the next lot. You probably mistook the number in your catalogue."

"I merely wanted one to sit on, sir."

"So do most of us, Pook. What else can one do with a chair?"

"I mean to borrow any chair to rest on, sir."

"You are ill then? No doubt the case of the Constable painting rests heavily upon your shoulders and is taking its toll."

"I've had an accident, sir."

"Excellent. Now may we proceed with the sale please?"

"Of course, sir."

"Thank you. Mind you don't set fire to my No Smoking sign with that flame-thrower you employ to light your pipe."

I struggled to compose myself for the bidding despite the terrible predicament I was in. I forced my features into an ingratiating smile necessary to convince Mr Mellon I was not greedy on two counts. First, that I did not insist on having all goodies knocked down to me, and second, that I did not think those goodies should be almost free. I called it my un-selfish smirk, indicating how we were all brothers in the trade, helping one another and forming a common defence wall against the public.

Nothing united the dealers into a brotherhood so much as seeing our very life-blood flowing to the Gentiles. Bernie Edelstein had gone so far as to request Mr Mellon to conduct his sales by ticket only, thus excluding the public from a public auction. It was outrageous, he said, that any passer-by could walk into a public auction and virtually snatch the bread from the mouth of a dealer who had been struggling to make an honest living for the past twenty-five years. Mr Mellon was probably breaking the law, he considered. What would the miners do if the public were permitted to enter a mine and pick their own coal, he demanded? Pull every miner out on strike and bring down the Government, that's what.

It had been an awful night with Sonia—my head reeled just to recall so much flesh, like being wooed by a whale and suffocated in the process. "I'm not just a pretty face you know, Peter," she had informed me superfluously as she unveiled the rest. But the nightmare was not over just by one shift on the treadmill of love. According to Sonia I was a perfect swine—such a perfect swine that I would have to visit her every night to prove I was truly serious about the alibi and not merely using her as a one night stand, seeing how men could never be trusted. Then I realized that in her broad country dialect she was calling me her perfect swain.

To make matters worse Tora had been round again, whereupon Olga had explained to her as woman to woman that we were an antique shop, not an appointments bureau for lonely hearts, and that Olga would ensure I kept the modelling date even if she had to wheel me round to the studio stuck on a plinth.

Olga herself had been dropping little hints that soon she would be taking that month's holiday in Oil-land with Yosseff by telling me she would leave my dinner in the oven, consisting of thirty-one pork pies from the supermarket, and to reserve Sundays for washing up the dishes.

There were also reminders of Olga on the catalogue. The next item due to come up—Lot 36: Set of four Regency sabre leg dining chairs in rosewood, red and white striped seats—was brought to my attention by a pen drawing of a felon hanging from a gibbet. Oddly enough he had been executed still smoking a pipe. Lot 42: George the First fruit-wood dressing-table on tapering legs with pad feet was marked by a delightful little sketch of a grave and headstone, clearly inscribed with the initials P.P.

Other items were similarly emphasized. Flicking through I noted a duelling-pistol at my head, the skull-and-crossbones resting upon my supine body, a Red Cross ambulance rushing me off the page, and eight tiny dealers carrying a coffin on their shoulders. Was she trying to tell me something, I wondered?

I won the sabre leg chairs for £35. Looking back I think Mr Mellon was kind to me, knocking them down fast so I would have plenty to sit on, giving me a set of chairs to make me better as other men might give me a brandy. He disapproved of dealers who passed away during a sale because it took folk's minds off the bidding and made them think of death and the futility of worldly possessions. I recall when Frank Owen Senior succumbed to a heart attack whilst bidding for a Sheraton harewood cylinder desk-bookcase with a tambour front, Mr Mellon had us stand in silence for two minutes as he intoned something about mortal man auctioning deceased owners' effects, yet now the bidder himself had suddenly joined the vendor at the Eternal Auction-Room in the sky—so it was incumbent upon him to re-offer the Lot to those who were still with us.

My luck held on Lot 42, the fruitwood dressing-table with pad feet merely because I continued to nod my head dazedly although I had lost track of the bidding. "How much did I pay, sir?" I cried, hearing that it had been knocked down to me.

"Shold to Mishter Pook at forty-pun," the ancient clerk informed me without looking up from his ledger.

The next target was Lot 45: a Regency demi-lune card table in satinwood, circa 1827, which Olga was anxious to purchase because she liked such terms as demi-lune, ormolu and sacristy to add tone to our shop. But Bernie Edelstein was bent on seizing this piece, visibly sweating, catalogue atremble and bidding with his teeth. Urged on by the hearse and coffin sketched on my own catalogue I did my best to stay with him but I dared not exceed £35. Bernie took the prize with a rounding-off call of £40, then favoured me with a yah-boo grin of triumph.

I smiled delightedly to let Mr Mellon see what a good loser I was and sportingly patted Bernie on the back exactly where I sometimes thought I might have to knife him one day.

"We can't have it all, can we, Pook?" Mr Mellon chuckled, wiping his glasses while the next lot was put up.

"We don't get it all either, sir," I chuckled back, to remind the old fool that I couldn't run my business on sympathy.

"But we mustn't be greedy, eh Pook?"

"Plenty for everyone, sir, as you always tell us."

"A fair price for a fair lot, that's our motto, Pook."

"That ideal will come one day, sir, as you so rightly say. Hope I live to see it."

"Remember, Pook, that in this hall we witness Nature's wonderful law of supply and demand, whereby every article finds its own price."

"Is that why it's so expensive, sir?"

"Each man offers what he thinks that article is worth to him."

"And goes home with nothing, sir. I tried it."

"So he must bid a little more than the next man."

"Then goes bankrupt, sir. The next man was bidding too high anyway."

"Sometimes, admittedly, a man is carried away by the exuberance of the sale-room atmosphere and overbids himself, Pook."

"Carried away by his friends to hospital, sir. Realizes he's paid £10 for a bucket, then finds a hole in it."

"Are you by any chance grumbling, Pook?"

"Oh no, sir, A good dealer never grumbles, sir. He learns to take the rough with the smooth and what he loses on the swings he makes up on the roundabouts. He is not the only pebble on the beach, sir, so he must take defeat in his stride and think how excellent it is to help his brothers-in-trade just as they yearn to help him. Above all, sir, he must always clear his junk after the sale and not leave bamboo pot-stands or rolls of worn lino behind."

Mr Mellon beamed. "First class, Pook. Who taught you such sound precepts of the business?"

"You did, sir. Every week. But we never tire of them because they mature like good wine. You always present them in a fascinating new light so they come out sparkling."

The porter was now displaying the next treasure for our delight, Lot 46: *The Boxer Rising* in eight volumes. A groan went up from the dealers at the sight of so much print.

"Must have been a hard contest, sir," I exclaimed, "if it took him eight volumes to get up."

Mr Mellon removed his spectacles to observe me better. "Not boxing, Pook. The great Chinese rebellion of 1900. Ladies, gentlemen and Mr Pook—the celebrated authority on historical ignorance—what am I offered for this magnificent set of learned tomes?"

"Sympathy," cried an unidentified voice.

"Imagine your whole family seated round the fire, engrossed in this monumental work."

"Watching it burn, sir?" I inquired.

"To make this lot even more attractive we have added three Ex-Army meat mincers and one gallon of Government Surplus creosote."

"Take a dollar, Guvner," Wally droned sadly.

"Ignoring the voice of doom, ladies and gentlemen, who will make me a reasonable offer which does not smack of charity?"

There followed that ominous silence of the auction during which time people turn round to look about them for no apparent reason unless it be to ascertain who is being silent.

"Take a dollar, Guvner," Wally moaned hopelessly.

"Surely, Mr Pook, this lot is worth one pound of anybody's money?" Mr Mellon questioned me dramatically.

I nodded agreement. "Stock a small shop at that, sir."

"Sold to Mr Pook for one pound," Mr Mellon snapped. "Next lot please, porter."

"Shold to Mishter Pook for one-pun," cried the clerk, writing aloud.

"Thank you, sir," I smiled bitterly. "Just what I've always wanted for my bedside table. Now I can read for six or seven hours before I drop off to sleep each night."

"Do I detect a hint of dissatisfaction, Pook?"

"On the contrary, sir, bliss. Take the rough with the smooth, you advised us, sir. This is the smooth. No jamjars or jelly-moulds." I immediately registered connoisseur's euphoria to let Mr Mellon see I was the happy dealer chuckling over my lot, as we say in the trade, even over Lot 46.

"Mind you clear the junk then, Pook."

"Always my first chore, sir. Junk first, then the perks. Leave the sale-room nice and tidy for the porters."

"Creep!" Bernie needled me.

Being affable to Uncle Mellon and laughing uproariously at his jokes on a wet Monday morning could be quite a strain, but I had mellowed since the old days of blazing rows in the sale-room, calling Mr Mellon a deaf old cheat and throwing my catalogue at him. I had learned the folly of ripping off a chair-leg and spraying the audience with woodworm powder when a chair was knocked down to me honeycombed like a dart-board.

"Capital, Pook, capital," Mr Mellon commended me. "Remember what the good book says—To him that hath shall be given."

"I didn't know that was actually in your Auction Handbook, sir."

"So, Pook you hath *The Boxer Rising*, and the meat-mincers and creosote hath been given unto you."

"Until my cup runneth over, sir. Imagine, one whole gallon!"

Mr Mellon removed his glasses in order to address the ceiling. "Now, ladies and gentlemen, another collector's piece—Lot 47: this important sauceboat in silver, 11½ ounces, by Thomas Farrer. Period George the Second, circa 1730. What am I offered for this magnificent example of the silversmith's craft?"

Lot 47 was marked in my catalogue with a sketch of a man on the rack shouting "Olga, have mercy on me!" because Yosseff often called her his incomparable little sauceboat and wanted to buy one as a souvenir of his wit, so I had to be on my toes.

"Er . . . I will offer . . . er . . . ten pounds, please," cried a lady wearing the fruits of the vine on her hat and waving her lorgnettes agitatedly to attract the auctioneer's attention.

The dealers turned on the Gentile with bared teeth, murmuring oaths against this interloper. "Thank you, madam, for opening the bidding for me," Mr Mellon bowed with old-world courtesy.

"Eleven," I snapped professionally.

"Thank you—fifteen pounds here from Mr. Pook. Who will raise it to twenty?"

"But I didn't. . . ."

"Ah, excuse me, ladies and gentlemen; my clerk has reminded me that the vendors wish this to be made a Combined Lot. You will be glad to learn that a delightful cuddly teddy-bear has been added to the silver sauceboat. An ideal present for any little toddler this Christmas."

"A teddy-bear!" I gasped. "You've actually put a teddy-bear in with a Georgian sauceboat!"

"We are assured that variety is the spice of life, Mr Pook."

"Where is this blessed teddy-bear then?"

"We conceal nothing, as you well know, Pook. The teddy-bear is on public display in the entrance lobby for the whole world to see and examine."

"I should like . . . er . . . to submit an offer of . . . er . . . twenty pounds, please," cried the nervous lady outlaw.

The dealers scowled and gnashed their teeth at the enemy. "Twenty-one," I called.

"I have twenty-five from Mr Pook down here. Do I hear thirty?"

"No," I squeaked falsetto without moving my lips.

Mr Mellon leaned over his rostrum like a ship's figurehead, hand cupped to ear in conventional listening pose. "May I tempt you with thirty, madam?" he cooed archly as though he were her lover. "Please don't lose this lovely objet d'art for the sake of a mere five pounds, I beg of you."

The lady was obviously confused, holding animated council with another lady. "Knock it down," I shouted impatiently. Olga had marked the catalogue £30 max; I was already on £25 but if the fruit hat went thirty my next bid must be £35. Even then Bernie Edelstein might be playing the eleventh-hour bid routine on behalf of the ring, striking his blow when the fruit hat and I had exhausted one another.

Mr Mellon was struggling. The fruit hat had obviously been advised by the floral hat not to risk going higher, Bernie was studying the *Racing Outlook* and everybody else was introvert.

"Madam, I pray you will secure this gorgeous period sauce-boat in finest Georgian silver by one of our mastercraftsmen. May I tempt you with twenty-six pounds, knowing that you will not lose it for one paltry pound—a mere twenty shillings."

The lady bandit nodded nervously, smiling gratefully at the romantic figure on the rostrum.

"Twenty-seven," I snapped. So now the old devil had reverted from fives to oncers. Surely he wouldn't tempt her next time with tanners?

"Ah, I have thirty from Mr Pook down here," Mr Mellon announced triumphantly. "Who will offer me thirty-five?"

I laughed delightedly at Mr Mellon's sharp stratagem, catching his eye and chuckling into it with heaving shoulders and wet cheeks to let him see I was a good sport who loved to be done, at the same time wondering if I set fire to his rostrum would he burn with it or would the heat force me back until he escaped.

"What fun it is with the gavel in your hands, sir," I giggled. "Never a dull moment here, sir, not like those boring old-fashioned auctions where you know where you are with the rules. This sale is as exciting as a casino. You may go down to posterity as the first auctioneer to raffle the lots, sir."

Mr Mellon glared unromantically at me. "Correct me if I err, Pook, but do I understand you are grumbling?"

"A good dealer does not know the word, sir. What better than to sit here amidst all the fun of the fair while you gallantly assist the ladies, sir? I say where else can you sit for the price of a sixpenny catalogue and watch a great actor perform? Next week *Hard Times*, eh!"

Mr Mellon drilled me with the left eye, reserving his right eye for the ledger. "Sold to Mr Pook for thirty-five pounds!" he roared, smacking the rostrum with his hammer in lieu of my head. "Don't forget to collect your teddy-bear too. Next lot, porter, or we shall never get through the day's programme."

Before I could protest Bernie Edelstein whispered in my ear, "So glad you won the teddy, Peter. Now at last you can give Olga something for Christmas. Herr-herr-herr-herr-herr!"

I had never heard Bernie laugh before. It scared me.

9

Olga screamed when she saw the giant Russian bear drag me into the shop and hurl me to the floor like a doll. All seven feet of the brute towered over me, wild-eyed, piano key teeth bared and those terrible claws poised high for the kill.

I held the monster off with my legs until I regained sufficient strength to rise and grapple with him once more, burying my face in his fur and shouting at Olga for help. But in seconds the bear had forced me backwards across the counter after we had staggered right round the shop locked in uneven contest. Olga was bravely hovering in the background holding high our anti-bandit cosh we kept by the till, screaming at me to be careful not to get hurt and exhorting me to turn the bear round so she could stun it from behind.

"It's stuffed!" I shrieked back lest I got coshed through mistaken identity or Olga's habit of squeezing her eyes shut before striking. "Don't hit it—help me keep it upright."

"It's stuffed!" Olga cried with feminine intuition. "I thought it was a real bear, Peter."

"It is a real bear but it's stuffed. Don't try to hold it up, woman—get behind and hold me up. It always topples forward and flattens you, see. I discovered this getting it into the trailer because the porters had to lift it off me five times, including once in the gutter outside the sale-rooms."

Olga shrieked again. "You actually bought that monstrosity

at the auction!"

"I had to. Mellon put it in with the Georgian sauceboat you wanted as a combined lot, dear. I got it for thirty-five pounds like you said, so really we haven't paid anything for the bear."

"But what possessed you to bid at all, knowing we would get lumbered with this King Kong, idiot?"

"Mellon said it was a cuddly teddy-bear for a toddler, dear."

"Did you have a seven-foot bear when you were a child? Is this what you hugged in your cot?—a full-sized Russian bear that could tear a horse to pieces. Did you think this was a teddy? Mr Mellon said it was a teddy so you bought it. If he showed you a palm tree and called it celery I suppose you'd eat it."

At last I finished my macabre waltz with the huge brute by allowing myself to be pinned in a corner, then dropping to the floor so that the bear leaned against the two walls. "I hadn't seen the bear, Olga. Mellon said it was on display in the entrance lobby so I had to take it on trust."

"Didn't you complain to the old chiseller for conning you?"

"Indeed I did, dear. I told him the teddy wasn't so much on display in the entrance lobby as blocking it completely. Then I said he was guilty of misrepresentation."

"What did he say to that, Peter?"

"Went off the deep end. Never thought he'd live to see the day when his dealers had lost their sense of humour and could no longer take a joke. Had it come to this, that an auctioneer was on oath while he handled hundreds of lots per day? Was he to conduct the proceedings as if he were a judge at a murder trial? Was I trying to kill the joy and excitement of the saleroom? How would I like to be banned again, as I was when I threw the Tompion bracket-clock at Bernie Edelstein and overturned the rostrum? How would I fancy six months suspension this time? Had the Constable painting gone to my head, sending me crazy with the lust for power?"

"Was he cross?"

"Cross! It was like being excommunicated by the Pope. He wouldn't let me have the sauceboat or anything else until I had loaded the bear. He even hinted that in his young days a recalcitrant vendee would have been flogged across the rostrum."

"So you immediately bent over, I suppose?"

"No, Olga. He set me a test joke and if I laughed hard enough he promised not to suspend me *sine die*. He said that meant until I die of sin."

"Let's have the joke and get it over with."

"He made me say 'I cannot bear not to bear my bear away'."

"And you laughed at that?"

"Hysterics, Olga. Cried into the fur until he reinstated me. How could I face you otherwise, dear? Besides, we got the bear free."

"If you tell me once more that we got this nightmare creature free I shall scream. What am I supposed to do with it?—cook it for lunch?"

"We'll sell it, darling. Sell it for £35, then we've got the sauceboat free and you can vamp it to Yosseff for £70—all profit."

Olga widened her huge brown eyes bearwards. "And who is going to buy the king of the jungle, pray? 'Suit council flat.

Ideal room-divider or would support ceiling. Not suitable children.' "

"Lots of people collect stuffed animals, dear."

"Lots of people who don't visit our shop—not that they could get in here any more."

"Listen, love, once I've stabilized its feet so it towers over you leaning backwards let me display it in the window for one week and I guarantee to sell it."

"Tora won't buy it—the fur covers the flesh."

"All I ask is one week, that's all."

"Well, we certainly shan't sell anything else with Big Foot filling the window. Not exactly the draw of the week, I'd say. Constable Barrington will come in to see our X certificate."

Not often Olga was wrong when it came to business matters. Our giant Russian bear drew a permanent small crowd to the window. The adults soon passed by but the children loved it and stayed for hours, many with their heads upside down, the better to examine its structure. Olga's sole correct prediction was that I couldn't sell it. In fact I learned how this nation of animal lovers is singularly anti-bear, classing it with elephants, whales and similar mammals which do not go well in the average lounge. Nor did the public take kindly to my sales talk that it was a cultural substitute for television, being larger, quieter and licence-free. I even invented a little bear history, telling how it had been shot by the Tsar of Russia in 1908 and until recently had been kept at the Imperial Bear Museum in Leningrad.

"Funny," remarked one client. "Never knew the Tsar of Russia ever went hunting in Canada." I couldn't figure out what he meant. But I found that I too was becoming anti-bear, sometimes peering through the window to snarl at it as it bared its fangs at me. On two occasions I would swear on oath that it actually roared at me in angry defiance; once when I raised my claws and bellowed a kind of territorial claiming growl at it, and once when I called it Winnie the Pooh.

The bomb scare came just after midnight. The noise made Olga scream out slightly ahead of me. Both of us lay there trembling.

"We've been bombed!" Olga cried.

"Perhaps it was next door. You know how they row at night."

"Row! It was either a bomb or a truck has run into the shop. I can still hear falling glass."

"Could it be a war film on their television, dear? You know how thin the walls are."

"Television! If the room was on fire you'd say it was a sudden heatwave. You're the man of the house, Peter—get up and find out before we're all murdered in our beds."

"Now? In the dark?"

"Don't let's wait for a bank holiday."

Boldly, without a trace of panic, I slid slowly from the bed, grabbed our anti-bandit cosh and threw on my pyjamas. I crept calmly to the window and looked out.

"Nothing, Olga," I reassured her. "Probably a nightmare after those fish and chips we had late."

"Draw back the curtains and look, idiot."

Coolly I parted the curtains to peer below. "There's been an accident, dear," I informed her.

"There'll be another accident in this room if you don't open the window and look properly."

Fearlessly I threw up the window sufficiently to take my head. "Heavens, Olga, there seems to be a man lying across the pavement wearing a fur coat."

"Sounds to me more like a man lying in his teeth. Stick your head right out."

"Yes, it's a huge man stretched across the pavement. The odd thing is that he seems to be surrounded by furniture. I'd better phone for an ambulance."

"I'll phone, Peter—you go out and help him."

While Olga dialled 999 I courageously went downstairs to the street. In the monlight I could see there had been a serious accident because our main window had been knocked out and the driver was lying prone on the pavement with his head in the road. I looked up and down the street but there was no sign of a car so I assumed the man was a pedestrian who had been the victim of a hit-and-run motorist—probably drunk and too scared to stop.

Picking my way through the furniture I reached the man in the fur coat, but when I knelt down to render first-aid I discovered he had a fur face as well. And a fur head.

"Dr Jekyll and Mr Hyde!" I screamed. "This must be another Mr Hyde!"

"'Allo, 'allo, 'allo, what have we here then?" a familiar voice inquired. I found it was Constable Barrington at my side.

"Jekyll and Hyde, remember? This looks like a similar case. Feel this horrible furry face, Constable—isn't it vile?"

Constable Barrington put his hand to my face and agreed. "You sure are, Pook, but never thought you'd admit it to me, of all people."

"I mean the monster. See, a man has turned himself into

131

a monster, just like in the book."

"Turned hisself into a bear, more like. That stuffed bruno of yours must have tried to escape and gorn through the winder. Shufti it yourself if you don't believe me."

Constable Barrington shone his torch so that the glass eyes blazed triumphantly at me. "Expect you finds that un-bearable, eh Pook?" he chuckled.

We were interrupted by the strident braying of the ambulance siren in search of accident-fodder. "Too late, mate," Constable Barrington told the driver, "he's dead."

"Take him away just the same, please," I begged. "Park him in the morgue—or anywhere."

"Sorry, mate, we only handle human stiffs. That's an RSPCA job. Night-night."

"Are you insured against damage, Pook?" Constable Barrington asked, surveying the wreckage that had once been our Nostalgia boutique.

"Not against Olga," I groaned sadly.

Constable Barrington leered meaningfully at me in the moonlight. "If you arsts me, Pook, Olga is the least of your worries when it comes to female dalliance—or whatever it is you calls meddlin' with other men's wives and daughters like."

It took me a long time to live down the bear fracas. Olga declared she would never forgive me even when the insurance company paid for a new window. She took on the role of Goldilocks to my three bears, greeting me at breakfast with such questions as "Who's been sleeping in *my* porridge?" and similar jibes.

She often told me I was not the Henry Ford of the antique's world, nor could she foresee us establishing a business empire

with branches across the land and subsidiary companies overseas. I did my best to impress upon her how all the celebrated
tycoons of commerce were failures in the beginning, whereupon she insisted that they were not failures all the time; that
there came a point where they started to be successful. She
asked me to name any business magnate who failed at the
beginning, grew worse, then ended up bankrupt. I refused to
answer, preferring to preserve my dignity by calling on Mrs
McGee.

Olga referred to this lady as Mrs McGee the First because
there were five McGees listed in our Inquiries book, all at
different addresses. This address fascinated me—Cliffhanger
Castle, Half-Horseball Magna, Cudfordshire. I discovered the
coast road leapt upwards out of the southern end of Half-
Horseball Magna at a ridiculous gradient which made one
feel that the car must topple backwards, then, two thirds of
the way up, I had to swing full-lock to the left off the main
road in order to traverse a kind of ledge along the cliff face.
This precarious track led nowhere except to Cliffhanger
Castle.

Owing to the nature of its position Cliffhanger Castle had
no option but to be a very small castle indeed; little more
than a cottage with ornamental battlements and a brass
cannon pointing seawards to command the ocean with its
neat pyramid of shot no larger than iron golf-balls. As a
precautionary measure I put the car in gear, then walked to
the door and banged its brass dolphin to announce my successful discovery of Mrs McGee's residence.

"Good-day, madam. I believe you wish to dispose of an old
sofa," I beamed, giving Mrs McGee my traditional trade
greeting, which always gave the impression that I came to

133

provide an essential service for the client's good, like a doctor or Meals-on-Wheels.

"And several other knick-knacks of various kinds, Mr Pook," she replied. "Do come in for a cup of tea."

Elderly Mrs McGee was not easy to understand because she spoke with that excess of gum work which accompanies no teeth, so that at first I suspected her of repeating the phrase 'mango chutney' between words.

"Are you related to the other McGee families who are selling up, madam?" I inquired, casing the joint for booty.

"Yes, all selling up to emigrate. Five families in all. Our daughter Eileen wants to gather us together in our old age. She thinks its better that way so we can all die as one big happy family."

"In Australia?"

"No, young man, London. Camden Town, where we all came from originally."

"How did you find your way here then?"

"Oh, by ship. My Albert was a coastguard and this place used to be a coastguard's cottage. Then we bought it and turned it into a castle. My Albert used to say that every man's home is his castle—so let's do the job properly."

While Mrs McGee poured the tea I looked round fascinatedly. The building was certainly open-plan, having this one main room and a kitchen on the ground floor, while immediately behind me was the ladder staircase. There was no banister, merely a stout knotted rope hanging down from the landing for support. Those windows which would no longer close tightly were permitting ivy to grow into the room. But I had long since learned to ignore people's domestic arrangements having once bargained with a lady across the body of her intoxicated spouse, and done business with a gentleman who wore a live cobra in his lounge.

I spilled some of my tea because I was so excited, and the reason I was so excited was the settee I sat on. I knew for sure it was none other than a Louis XVI conversation settee, carved and painted in the grand manner. It stood on eight legs, and was some eight feet in length because a conversation settee has two semi-armchairs let in behind the main seat to allow a group of people to chat among themselves over their shoulders. My professional eye dated the prize at around 1780—nine years earlier than the French Revolution.

Every time Mrs McGee returned to the kitchen I was under the couch like a ferret, checking for stability, woodworm and general condition. Apart from spring sag and worn upholstery —no problem at all in the trade—it appeared to be perfect. Given a fortnight Vic Armstrong and Mr Bentley would have it looking as though it had come straight from the original cabinetmakers in Paris. Advertised in the right journals such as *Country Life* it must fetch £500, possibly more at a quality auction. Instinctively I shoved the cat off it.

Like any dealer worth his salt I was quite happy to do business here with a green and yellow parakeet perched on the top of my head, so I sat there wearing my Wildlife Trust smile. Apparently Captain Kidd had recently belied his sex by laying an egg, according to my hostess, so I felt certain he had laid a second one on my forehead until she handed me a cloth to wipe it off.

The combination of tea, cakes and treasure made me quite nauseous. There were rarities dotted everywhere one turned. On the mantleshelf reposed a glass Victorian paper-weight that snowed when turned, already becoming valuable in collectors' circles; chased fire-irons rested across a shining pierced brass fender; copper based silver tankards hung from hooks in the oak beams; two silver chambersticks with snuffers stood on a window-ledge; a Regency brandy warmer and a Victorian silver sugar basket with blue glass liner decorated a wall-shelf; a Queen Anne lidded pewter tankard caught my eye.

The Welsh-dresser made me quite dizzy to perceive. It seemed to be loaded with china, from Belleek to Coalport, from Copeland to Dresden, from Doulton to Derby, from Minton to Moorcroft. I feared I might faint at the sight of so much booty, glancing round apprehensively for signs of those two enemies to our profession—nosy neighbours and greedy relations. Yet here, I thought to myself, was one place where I had no competition. I clutched a Staffordshire dog to re-assure myself it was not a dream.

Another astonishing thing was the way in which Mrs McGee priced her possessions, for whatever I offered she either accepted gladly or chided me for being too generous. At each deal she shouted aloft to her husband, "Fancy that, Albert! This kind young man is going to pay us hard cash for the junk poor mother left you!"

Gradually a feeling stole over me for the first time in my career that, little as it was, I was paying too much. When I suggested £1 for a late Georgian mahogany corner washstand with marble top, Mrs McGee roared with glee, throwing back her head to call up the ladder-staircase, "Hark at this, Albert! One whole sovereign for Aunt Amanda's old washstand! I'm sure the young man's crazy!"

So when it came to the conversation settee I had reduced my bid to £5, and even then the lady begged me to think again before I threw good money after bad. Just as I was consulting my conscience if I dare offer thirty shillings for a Louis XVI collector's showpiece without being punished by the Almighty for unarmed robbery, Mrs McGee bawled upstairs, "You'll never believe this, Albert, but Mr Pook wants to pay a fiver for that tatty old sofa which was here when we first come, remember? Such an uncomfortable thing too. He's been so good with all our other rubbish—shall we let him take it away for nothing?"

Then Mrs McGee turned to me. "I do hope you don't let the rest of our family take advantage of you when you visit them, Mr Pook. You see, I must warn you that they're a bit different to us. How can I put it? They're just a little bit odd —eccentric, you might say. They might even try to do you, especially when they find out you're so generous with your cash."

I knew it was all a dream; that any moment I should wake up in bed at home, sweating and dazed. The nature of our trade—this incessant search for treasure—often gave me that occupational disease known as dealer's indigestion, nightmares born of cupidity I had learned to dread. Sometimes I entered a kind of Aladdin's Cave stacked with objets d'art for the taking, followed by the heavy endless labour of carting it away, yet always running back for more. Or I was attending an auction where nobody made a bid for any lot except me, and once again I sweated through hundreds of lots lest I lose a single item.

One of my worst dreams located me in the grounds of Chatsworth House. There was a great fire within and the fire-brigade chief told me I could have all I could save. Henceforth I resembled an Olympic sprinter shuttling between the art treasures and my awaiting pantechnicon, rushing from the house like furniture with feet, then returning exhausted for more loot. When I had managed to transport a grand-piano single-handed from the Music Room to my van I collapsed at last, to awake on the floor of my bedroom with mild delirium.

Worst of all was the Investiture at Buckingham Palace, where the Queen was knighting me for services to Britain. "I name you Sir Peter Pook," the Queen announced graciously. "I confer upon you the Order of the Wardrobe— which on no account are you to sell. I am pleased to say you have sold more antiques abroad than any living man, thus helping Britain's exports to the extent that only British Leyland, Ford and ICI have exceeded your figures."

"Thank you, your majesty," I purred. "It was nothing really—just the luck of the draw coupled with hard work, expertise, initiative, courage and superhuman greed. I shall do even better next year."

The Queen smiled approvingly. "Splendid, Sir Peter! As a token of my esteem I wish you to choose as many art treasures as you please from the royal apartments, provided that you do not dally more than one hour. Goodness gracious, Sir Peter has run off from my presence!"

Then the terrible business would start again of stripping the palace in one hour flat, running out to my pantechnicon with grandfather clocks under my arms and console tables on my head, sprinting back into the palace to drag a whole roomful of furniture to the van by means of the carpet it stood upon, eventually to awake panting and feverish to discover I was hauling the covers off the bed.

By this method over the years I stripped the Victoria and Albert Museum, Blenheim Palace, Windsor Castle, The Tower of London, Longleat House, Sandringham, and several other repositories of antiquity. Once I even managed to display the *Mona Lisa* in one window of our shop and the Elgin Marbles in the other. On another occasion after a party a large crowd thronged our premises to view the Crown Jewels. More than once I would be strolling along the road when such items as a mahogany barometer by James Gatty and Georgian silver wine-coolers would tumble undamaged from the back of a lorry, which I picked up and hurried home with. I recall finding a box of silver vinaigrettes in this manner—one gross of them to be exact.

Thos. Snuff, of Snuff Bros., often warned me how dealer's indigestion was a danger signal that one had been in the trade too long and could lead to the dreaded Little Nells. Those of our profession who succumbed to the Little Nells manifested the disease in several ways. For example, no matter where you were or what the occasion you picked up everything you saw, turned it over and examined the bottom with a reading-glass. This could be particularly embarrassing when invited to dinner and found yourself scrutinizing the bottom of a sauce-boat for china marks with a lapful of gravy. Thos. Snuff even did this when they handed him his first grandson.

Old Samuel Gruntling, who had been born at the back of an antique shop like kittens and was now pushing ninety, refused to unlock his shop door because he could no longer bear the public coming in and purchasing his treasures. One side of his door card read: NEVER OPEN. When he reversed it at closing time it read: CLOSED FOR EVER.

But this dream did not end. It merely got better and better. Every instinct in my body told me to flee with my new trophies, so I paid up over a full written receipt. Next, I packed the goods, glass and china well strawed in tea-chests, furniture padded with old blankets I always carried. There remained only the conversation settee, for which I had reserved the giant roof-rack.

After ten minutes I had come to the conclusion that coastguards of old must have been dwarfs because the settee refused to go through the door and was obviously too large for the window. I wondered if they had brought the settee into the cottage via the roof before the thatch had been put on. I was an expert furniture-mover but the settee would not respond to any of the stock manœuvres, such as standing it on end then sliding the back and seat around the doorpost with a minimum of space.

As I sweated to force an eight-foot settee through a six-foot door and became trapped in its eight legs and auxiliary armchairs as though it was an upholstered octopus, I conceived a wild idea of fetching a cold-chisel and four-pound hammer for widening Mrs McGee's entrance by twelve vital inches. The only other solution would involve sawing off three legs, but five-legged settees are difficult to market.

Hearing those terrible triple-oaths essential to this type of operation Mrs McGee hurried in from the kitchen. "Won't it go through?" she inquired, pin-pointing my problem with feminine exactitude. "Why don't you leave the clumsy old thing and I'll chop it up for the fire."

I leaned against the wall to recover my breath. "Mrs McGee, If I promise to repair any damage would you permit me to knock part of this wall down? Only about a foot all the way down so I can swivel the legs round." Now I knew it was a dream. A week earlier I had purchased from a stall in Cudford Street Market an eighteenth-century Chinese goose soup-tureen for sixpence, which must fetch £3,000. But when I went to lift it, small as it was, I failed. Struggle though I might I could not shift a mere piece of china to carry it home. The street-traders laughed so loudly at my efforts that I woke up, absolutely convinced I was lying in a bed at Cudford General Hospital suffering from hernia.

So any moment now the form was for Mrs McGee to produce an electric saw, go through the settee like butter, then hand me a kind of Louis the Sixteenth furniture construction kit, saying, "Even a child can assemble this exciting do-it-yourself period sofa in half-an-hour. Full instructions inside box."

Instead, she said, "Bless my soul, Mr Pook, if you must hump it away why don't you use the window?"

"The window is even smaller than the door, Mrs McGee. Perhaps your bifocals mislead you."

"I mean the big 'un upstairs. Years ago 'twas the observation window, so 'tis a mighty wide 'un."

My heart leapt at the news. The banister-free stairs would present no problem. "Will Mr McGee mind?" I inquired courteously. What I really meant was will he mind if I have to lean across his bed and rip the window-frame clean out of the wall.

"Not a bit of it, Mr Pook. He don't mind what you do provided I'm happy."

"I suppose he couldn't give me a hand up the stairs?"

"Ah, I doubt if he'd be up to that, m'dear."

Laying a blanket on the ladder-stairs I heaved the settee up slowly but surely. The top floor of the cottage proved to consist of one room only, uncarpeted and containing little more than an iron bedstead. Even stranger, the bed was made and there was no-one occupying it.

"Is your husband about, Mrs McGee?" I asked puzzledly.

"No m'dear. He's dead."

"Dead!"

"Been gone these last twelve years."

"But I thought you were calling up to him."

"Of course. Consults him about everything I do. He was a good man—the very best—otherwise I would have to call down to him, see?"

"Does he answer?"

"You bet your life he do! Just like when he was a coast-guard. He may be dead but, believe me, he don't leave me alone in the cottage. He's always on duty, looking after me, he is."

Opening the big observation window I experienced a weird sensation that Mr McGee was keeping his eye on me too. At last I had found an aperture large enough to accommodate the settee quite comfortably, so, having balanced my treasure safely across the window-ledge with one end resting on a chair, I requested Mrs McGee to wait there with her husband while I went below.

The cottage was so small that a step-ladder sufficed to raise me outside to window level, where Mrs McGee gently eased the settee to me, sliding the back across the blanketed window-ledge. I had done it a hundred times before so I knew how to distribute the weight as more and more of the couch oozed out. Expertly I lowered the leading end down to the top of the step-ladder, gradually and delicately to avoid scratch marks. It was a professional job indeed.

There came a moment when the settee had to balance upright on the head of the step-ladder, so in order to provide me with essential support I gently eased my left foot from the ladder and across to the top of the little garden wall. It was not so much a wall as a wooden fence, but it supplied a firm foothold because I happened to be opposite a post. Now I had obtained sufficient stability to take the dead weight of the settee for lowering to the ground.

Olga asked me afterwards why I did not rope the settee down from the window. Well, the trouble with roping is that one man cannot support such a weight in such a position—two men are hard pushed—and secondly, it is impossible to prevent scraping damage down the brickwork. I should know, for I ruined a sideboard that way.

Mrs McGee's scream drowned mine as the green post snapped without warning. I swung outwards like a huge snail, wearing the settee on my back as it were. Fortunately I did not panic; there was not time for it. All I had to do was land as softly as possible from the inconsiderable height of a four-foot fence, but the big problem was to take and cushion the force of the settee when it followed me.

Hitting the long grass lightly, I immediately braced my body for the shock, prepared to accept any pain to save my prize. The settee descended with body-shaking velocity, though fortunately for me I was struck by the padded seat and padded back, yet so heavily that I was knocked off balance through the bushes. I tensed myself to break a second fall—but there was nothing to fall on.

Even as I somersaulted, my eyes could see enough to warn me that the McGee's garden did not extend beyond the bushes, for I was actually rolling down the sheer face of the cliff. Desperately I seized a bush, only to be buffeted by the settee with such violence that I went into a kind of orbit, bush in hand. Now I was performing back somersaults down the cliff, and at the apogee of each revolution I was enabled to glimpse Mrs McGee's enlarged eyeballs staring at me in disbelief and hear her voice imploring me to come back.

By some law of momentum unfamiliar to me, the settee had gone ahead but I was incapable of catching it up or halting my descent. In fact, several bulges on the cliff face accelerated my progress by literally throwing me outwards until I was fairly bouncing down. The settee was performing huge cartwheels in front of me, while I followed suit on a smaller scale, but to be honest I was now concentrating entirely, not on saving the settee, but on saving my life.

I did not tumble into the sea. I was flung into it as though Mr McGee was kicking me off Britain with his boot. I remember hitting the ocean with a tremendous double splash, then resurfacing to tread water and collect my wits. Two hundred feet above me I could distinguish Mrs McGee still paralysed at the bedroom window, unable to absorb what had happened so rapidly. Twenty yards beyond me floated the settee, partly submerged on the iceberg principle and obviously being carried out by the tide, as if determined to return to its country of origin. I tried swimming back to the cliff but the current was too strong for me, so I turned and chased the settee. As far as I knew, Mrs McGee was not on the phone so I waved desperate Mayday signals, pointing towards France to indicate my course and praying she would not go downstairs to make a cup of tea and forget about me.

10

Those marvellous men of the Royal National Lifeboat Institution have only one deficiency. They have not been trained to rescue furniture. Jim Connor, coxswain of the Cudford Lifeboat, merely grinned as I was lifted from the sea gasping, "Never mind me—save the settee!"

I clung to my treasure to the end, until it was waterlogged and submerged except for one castor. I was picked up over a mile south-west of Half-Horseball Magna, floating by using the settee for buoyancy and utilizing my free arm to wave landwards.

Jim Connor found it difficult to understand how an antique dealer could be so far from his natural habitat with his merchandise, but he kindly agreed to put down a marker-buoy for my future use. He found it even more difficult to believe my explanation that I had been moving the settee from a house and had fallen into the ocean. He had rescued so many holidaymakers who were carried out to sea while sunbathing on inflatable beds that he seemed to think the same thing had happened to me on an inflatable couch.

One advantage of falling into the sea and arriving home late was that Olga was out. She had left a note which read: 'Your dinner is in the oven. Have just popped over to Oilland. Don't wait up. Love, Olga.' I opened the oven and discovered thirty individually-wrapped pork-pies inside.

What a shame, I thought, that I was unable to display my treasure trove to her that I had unearthed at Mrs McGee's. In fact I had difficulty in displaying it to anyone at the moment because the fall had left me considerably bruised about the neck and back. Consequently, like the spider, I had to turn my whole body round to look behind, and to put on my shoes involved lying on the bed, then hooking them on from the rear.

Olga had once remarked that the Government would soon use me as an excuse for nationalizing the antique trade, but in my heart I believed I was a natural entrepreneur and the McGee Trove, as I referred to it, was proof of my talent.

Another person who believed in me was Tora, who came to see her idol on the morrow. She appeared surprised that Olga was not in the shop to chaperon me. I struggled to be sophisticated in her presence, though I was now compelled to sit bolt upright on a high chair whenever possible, rising slowly when required to move and gliding about the shop arched like a bow.

"You did not come for our modelling date, Peter," Tora purred accusingly.

"So sorry, Tora, but I've had an accident," I explained, to account for the fact that I did not normally sit before ladies with my face screwed up.

"An accident! How?"

"I was carrying a settee and slipped. Two hundred feet. You'll read about it in The Echo tonight. Fortunately I landed in the sea and the Cudford Lifeboat picked me up. Some folks are saying it was a publicity stunt."

"My Peter is hurt! This is terrible! But perhaps I can help you. I have been trained as a nurse. I will massage your poor body back to health. I will make you fit as a wild stallion. If all else fails I am qualified to give you acupuncture. The Chinese have an ancient adage: 'When you are sick a skilful prick will do the trick'."

"I'm only bruised, dear—not dying."

"I shall see Olga about nursing you back to virility."

"That will be difficult, Tora; she's gone abroad for a month's holiday."

"Excellent! There is no problem. I shall nurse you night and day till she returns. By then even she will not recognize you, darling. I shall be back directly I have collected my equipment."

That afternoon I realized how Tora's equipment consisted of three suitcases and a bag such as doctors carry. I hauled everything up to the bedroom as she ordered, under the impression it was some complicated physiotherapy apparatus for my treatment, but Tora opened the cases and began to hang dresses and other feminine attire in the wardrobe. When I protested she told me to stop worrying about myself and lie on the bed. How else could she manipulate my spine, massage me and generally tone up my body? I was not to talk because talking in my condition could be dangerous, drained one's reserves of energy and could lead to myelitis of the lumber medulla—even the dorsal and cervical. Whereupon I shut up like a clam.

"Lie still on your stomach and I will get to work on you, darling," Tora commanded in a most un-nurselike tone. "But first take everything off or I cannot reach your quadratus lumborum."

"Don't. . . ."

"Silence, Peter—remember? Try not to sap your strength

147

merely to thank me."

I felt extremely vulnerable, lying face-downwards on the bed and afraid to open my mouth. In Tora's bag I had spotted a set of acupuncture needles and I had read somewhere that they were seldom inserted in the seat of the pain but in the most unlikely places elsewhere. Or would Tora insert them in the seat of the patient, using the Norwegian harpoon method?

"You are just the case nurses love to handle," Tora informed me, pouring what I assumed was whale oil from a bottle on to my back. Then she began a delightful slippery massage until I imagined her as an octopus exploring a new rock.

"What a magnificent torso you have, Peter," she sighed. "You have muscles everywhere, and in some places there are muscles which are having their own muscles. They ripple like the waves of the ocean and when I am massaging them down here other muscles come up to look. I must warn you it is making me feel extremely—how you say in English?— sexipated. Never have I seen such an exciting sacrum nor felt such pulsating ilia."

"I didn't think they were anything special, dear." Anything special! I didn't even know I had them. How maddening, I reflected, to be so short of facial fruit yet going through life little suspecting I possessed a fascinating sacrum and unique ilia. I wondered if they were attributes one might show off at dances and other social occasions. Luckily I belong to that hard breed of men who are impervious to flattery and know exactly how far to let women go. I smiled superciliously to myself, quietly confident in the armour of my iron self-discipline.

Tora now plugged in the vibro-massager, gently running it up and down my spine till I was forced to cry out with tingling ecstasy. "Is your back feeling better already, darling?" Tora inquired.

"My back is great but the rest of me seems to have died," I gasped.

"Good. Then I will work all over you and bring the rest back to life. How fortunate I am here to care for you, cook for you, sew for you, mind the shop for you, do everything for you."

I lay silent while my mind sorted out this comprehensive aid programme. Any normal man would have jumped at the opportunity of having this leggy blonde ministering to his needs, but I was made of sterner stuff, high-principled, independent, tough, indifferent to sex, and, above all, a firm believer in revenge by suspicious minds. For instance, Olga's.

So I said calmly, concealing the iron fist beneath the velvet glove, yet masterfully and decisively, "Oh!"

"You shall know what it is to be a Viking hero, Peter, waited on body and soul by your willing slave-girl. I will be all things to you. Your bondmaid, your courtesan, your dancing-girl, your houri, your concubine."

"Imagine that on the income-tax returns!"

"For one month you will live as you deserve to live—as a king among men, served by your adoring slave."

"Are you sure you've come to the right address, Tora?"

"You will know what it is to experience that fantasy world other men can only dream of."

"But Olga. . . ."

"Do not fear, darling. You will sleep in your room, I shall occupy the front bedroom."

"But that is my room."

"Fancy that! How coincidence does rule our lives, my mighty Nordic god. It seems even Fate is determined to throw us together. There is no escape for us. I was born solely for your pleasure—master."

"Me!"

"Oh Peter, when will you listen to your nurse and stop arguing about everything, you naughty chatterbox? How can I make you better if you talk so much? Leave everything in my hands and all will be bliss—beyond your wildest dreams."

I could not absorb so much shock in my present condition. I needed time to think, to consider, to weigh the pros and cons.

"I am master in my own house, Tora," I decided firmly. "A serious affair like this cannot be rushed. I shall give you my decision first thing tomorrow morning."

Tora kissed my cervical vertebrae delightedly. "What a powerful master you are, Peter. A king indeed! Tell me in the morning before I make the tea."

As anyone knows only too well who has tried, it is impossible to run an antique's business single-handed. Two is the minimum; one to sell and one to buy. Unlike other trades, you cannot phone up the wholesalers and restock, nor does a salesman call every week asking if he can put you down for a dozen Dutch brass cauldrons with paw feet or a gross of silver mounted double horn powder-flasks. You desire all these things but you have to get around to find them; and, perhaps the saddest thought of all, search for them in an ever-diminishing market. It is the same story when they knock down beautiful old buildings—brother, there just ain't no more. Like the dodo they become extinct, beyond recall of anything beyond memory and legend.

This was the reason that I allowed Tora to stay put, otherwise out she would have gone, bag and baggage. I felt certain Olga would understand this vital business logic and would not suspect any ulterior motives. Ideally, of course, she wouldn't find out.

Life with Tora was unusual, to put it mildly. She explained how at school she had taken three years to make her cookery apron, by which time it did not fit her and the cookery class had ended anyway. Nevertheless we ate well. Tora employed the random method, whereby she served whatever was available whenever it was cooked. Once she roused me in the middle of the night so urgently that I automatically leapt from bed and grabbed our anti-bandit cosh, shouting, "Burglars!"

"No, darling—supper is ready at last," she explained.

But undoubtedly Tora's most disturbing habit was finding things like the hair-dryer. She would suddenly appear in the shop to ask me wearing only a towel-turban and high-heels. To combat this I developed a specialized survival technique whereby in one athletic leap I was able to seize and open an Empire period draught-screen to shield Tora's body from the public gaze. As an added precaution I walked with the screen enveloping her until she had left the shop. Finally, I replaced the screen in its permanent emergency position like a ship's lifebelt, then collapsed on a chaise-longue to fight off thoughts of what the future might hold for me.

Nobody could deny that Tora was good for business. In fact she seemed to lure men in as though we were running a clip-joint rather than a boutique, with the result that we sold merchandise to fellows who had never entered more than a pub and a betting-shop in their lives.

"Such lovely beddy men seem to live around Cudford," Tora explained after selling a Victorian singing bird in a brass cage to Butch McTaggart, a local wrestling idol. "I do find them so 'citingly sexipating. Butch has such a manny smell about him—I think his body is one mass of erotogenous zones."

"He certainly thought yours is, Tora."

But everything paled into insignificance beside Tora's hidden talent for the Beledi—which was about the only talent she did hide. I had already noticed how neighbours raised their brows and rolled their eyeballs when passing me in the street, as if acknowledging me as the local sultan who did not have to rely on television for his love life like ordinary men do. Therefore, as I stood in the bathroom examining my head for grey hairs it struck me as coincidental that eastern music should be emerging from below.

My years in the Middle East and Far East enabled me to recognize the urgent, plaintive wail of the Beledi—the rhythmic beat of the dumbeki, the metallic shake of the def tambourine, the lilt of the stringed saz. I listened to the music, pleased by the memories it invoked, until suddenly a new sound hit my ear. It was the insistent chiming of the zills, those tiny finger-cymbals whose volume far outweigh their size. Zills could mean only one thing—someone was belly-dancing downstairs.

Running into the shop I automatically got the screen round Tora, locked the door and lowered the window blinds almost in one practised operation. Then I switched off the stereo, and stood panting. "Tora, what are you doing?" I gasped superfluously.

She threw me a surprised smile. "I'll give you three guesses, darling. Start off with ice-skating."

"I mean what are you thinking of?—belly-dancing in the shop at high noon!"

"I am thinking of you, Peter, so I am belly-dancing in the shop for you too."

"But you just can't do that sort of thing, Tora."

"Oh but I can, darling. I have studied and learned the true traditional belly-dancing of the harem, not the rubbish one sees in comedy. I was taught by the great Saida-Soraya of Egypt, one of the world's most beautiful and skilled mistresses of the Beledi."

"She taught you in Egypt?"

"No, Peter, in Chigago. You see, the Beledi is sweeping America, for it enables woman to revive her femininity and mystery—and to hypnotize her man. It is the ancient dance of the womb—like so."

Tora raised her arms above the head to begin the most extraordinary undulations and rolls of the abdomen I had ever witnessed, causing her amber navel jewel to swing in a complete circle.

"That is my tummy drill but also I can do the same with the rest of my parts because every muscle has been trained to dance. I show you."

Switching on the stereo Tora began her routine barefoot, gliding gracefully round the carpet with a long yellow veil draped down her back so she could use the finger-cymbals. The silver coins sewn to the fringed green-and-orange brass top tinkled in movement, as did the gold coin belt set low on her hips. From the belt dropped an emerald green slit hip skirt of silk, covering transparent orange pantaloons beneath. Slender gold slave-chains hung loosely about her ankles. Each of her arms was embraced by coiled snake arm-bracelets, while her neck was swathed by a rich layered choker in gold. Her ears held dangle-hoop earrings almost to her shoulders. The long blonde hair completed a technicolor picture that fixed me bug-eyed in my tracks.

"You see, Peter, how modest is my ensemble," Tora remarked as she gyrated swivel hips and universal-jointed shoulders. "Only my midriff is exposed. Yet I hope you find me attractive."

Attractive! As a businessman who seldom gave women a second glance. I was surprised to discover myself staring as though I had lockjaw. "You're gorgeous, honey," I admitted.

"Then you do not mind if I keep up my belly-dancing, darling?"

"I hope I'm not narrow-minded, dear. As a man of the world I have always supported cultural pastimes and ethnic dances. Of course you can. All I ask is that you practise outside of shop hours and use another room."

"But, darling Peter, this is the only space big enough. Otherwise I should be forced to dance in the garden—or even outside in the street."

"Say no more, Tora. Use the shop after hours, but do make sure you pull the blinds first...."

Oddly enough, at that very word the roller-blind covering the shop door flew up of its own accord, revealing the bulky un-Eastern silhouette of Constable Barrington. Never had I seen his bloodshot eyes so large. Tora froze in mid-shake and called sensuously, "Welcome, my brave sheik, to the tent of thy favourite."

Constable Barrington removed the helmet from his head and wiped his thinning pate with a handkerchief. "Gawd lumee, Pook, what you done this time? Got your own 'arem?"

"This is my new assistant, Tora. She's merely . . . er . . . practising a traditional dance for the local church fete."

"Looks more like she's practising it for the local broffel— and don't tell me it's part of the Arab states' efforts to help underdeveloped countries like Britain."

"Purely cultural, I do assure you, Constable Barrington. Same as you used to do morris dancing on the village green."

"I walks me beat thinking how quiet things is lately, then what do I hear? Pook's nightclub in full blast. Jew know I could porridge you for not holding a singing and dancing licence? Jew know I could porridge you for change of user under the Town and Country Planning Act? Where's Olga, by-the-by?"

"Olga has gone abroad for a rest and holiday."

"Don't wonder at it with you as a partner. So you gets this tart in right away, eh? My oath, Pook, you don't waste no time, you don't."

"Ahhhhhh—you don't understand the position, Constable Barrington." This was a slow sentence with an extremely long Ah to give me alibi time, but it seemed to be half an hour too short.

Constable Barrington made those peculiar chest noises he thought were laughing. "Then just you tell the simple old-fashioned village flatfoot what the position is in short easy words he won't confuse with lyin'."

I dropped into full confessional pose with head bowed practically on the policeman's shoulder so Tora would not hear.

"Olga knows I can't run the business alone so she asked her sister to come in to tide us over the holiday period, you see."

"So this girl 'ere has just been born, eh?"

"How do you mean, Constable?"

"I mean that I knows, you knows, Olga knows and her mother Mrs Brown knows that she never had no sister. Three brothers yes, but none of them was female siblings. They weren't even poofy."

"Ahhhhhh—you don't know the full story, Constable."

"Nobody ever will if you speaks that slow, Pook. You never used to be a talking snail. Perhaps it's your forked tongue bothering you."

"Well, prepare yourself for a surprise, Constable."

"I'm going to hear the truth for once?"

"Tora is Olga's half-sister by a former marriage."

"Whose former marriage?"

"Mr Brown's."

"Well well, I never heard tell o' that!"

"The family always hushed it up, of course."

"Shot every witness?"

"Mr Brown married very young when he was stationed in Norway."

"Funny, seeing how he fought in the Desert Rats. "

"Ah—before the African campaign."

"Just after breakfast, I suppose?"

Sensing my discomfort, Tora glided over to the doorway and gave Constable Barrington her head-to-toe snake-down with all systems go. "I hope you are not cross with me, my handsome legionnaire. I am but a humble slave-girl trying to please her master in the market-place."

"Strewf!" Constable Barrington gasped. "In Cudford!"

"I know how in England there are many strange laws, such as forbidding the people to drink their beer in the afternoon, so you must tell me if it is wrong to dance in a house. If it is not illegal please may I dance for you, my bold gendarme?"

"Strewf! In Cudford!"

For the first time in my life I saw Constable Barrington retire baffled and at a loss for words. At last he seemed to have encountered a situation outside his realm of experience. He ambled off shaking his head puzzledly, obviously determined to remedy this defect in his knowledge by consulting the bye-laws at the station.

Tora practised her art every morning during our quiet period from nine to ten, for which I lettered a card to inform the public that 'This establishment is closed daily from nine to ten a.m. for the training of staff'.

Each day I retired to the workshop during these hours to renew my battle against the obdurate timbers of yesteryear, listening to the unfamiliar music of the East filtering through the door. My ears gradually grew accustomed to the slow Tcheftetelli, the improvised Taxim, the Maqam and the Indian Raga. I even began to identify individual instruments, such as the ney flute, the rabab and the stringed kemanche—which Tora had told me with a surprising gift of prophecy was liable to drive men to the ecstasy of temporary madness, like a drug.

Confidentially, this last was the reason I no longer watched Tora's performance, for, despite my strict upbringing, my family had not rendered me impervious to this ancient method of slowly driving men off their rocker. Nor had my school music mistress, Miss Ridling, warned me that certain instruments might deprive me of my self-control to the extent that required psychiatric treatment. It was certainly a far cry from my rendering of the *Fairyland Waltz* on her piano.

Running a business with Tora's assistance was one of the most exciting experiences of my life, developing in me a distinct bagginess about the eyes and a noticeable trembling of the hands. She insisted I model for her in the evenings in order to sculpt the statue that was to be submitted for her college degree, entitled *Dawn Man Seeks Mate*. To fulfil the spirit of this kind of prehistoric personal column advert I was required to pose on a concrete slab with my knees well bent outwards, while my right hand held a crude club essential to primeval courtship. My left hand shaded my eyes, the better to survey the land for signs of Dawn females suitable to my purpose. Tora told me I was the perfect model for the job, and all she had to do was pack cotton-wool along my gums to emphasize the anthropoidal features. Not that I let such typical feminine flattery go to my head, but it pleased me to think that I could well go down to posterity immortalized in cement alongside such masterpieces as *The Kiss* and *Adam*. Tora constantly praised my beauty of countenance and perfection of form, yet it was difficult to reconcile such eulogies with the fearsomely rapacious creature arising before my very eyes in nightly dollops of cement.

Two reminders of Olga arrived during this period in the shape of passionate camel-enriched postcards depicting the Middle East at its touristy best, informing me that she was having a high old time amidst unaccustomed luxury and generous friends. Only one worry was spoiling her holiday and that was the dread of it ending. She missed me very much, so she knew I would not mind if she took an extra week in order to visit Ka-El-Shakkem, but did not specify if it was a place or a man. Finally, I would be overjoyed to hear that she had learned to drive a camel, which, Yosseff assured her, had earned her the title among his friends of She Who Bounces Beautifully On Sand.

The crisis came five days before Olga was scheduled to stop bouncing and return to Cudford. I was chain-smoking in the workshop, listening to the rousing lilt of the Dabkie folk-dance with my toes curled as I sawed distraughtly through the cabriole leg on the bench, wondering if my present mode of life would lead to fits, when Tora began to emit erotic cries of Ayawah! Ayawah! so loudly that I feared it might be Arabic for Help.

I ran into the shop and what met my eyes caused me to keep running so as to whip the shop blinds down, lock the door and automatically get Tora screened up. Then I lay on the chaise-longue because I could no longer conceal the fact that I was a nervous wreck. They say worry is a killer, which would account for my legs dying on me. Nor could I speak for some time.

"I practise a new dance for you, Peter. It is very old, as old as history itself," Tora explained sympathetically.

"Sounds about as old as I feel."

"It is based on the dance Salome performed to please King Herod so he would give her John's head on a silver salver."

"Just like Olga will have mine. I could end up mounted on the wall, next to that stag's head."

Tora pouted red lips. "My wonderful Peter does not want me to dance? Slave-girl does not please her royal master?"

I waved my hands hopelessly. "That's not the point, dear. It's just that Cudford folk are old-fashioned and likely to gossip if they see you doing the Dance of the Seven Veils in the local shopping district. Some of them haven't recovered from the Cancan yet, and still whisper about Gay Paree. Mrs Edwards believes that Bingo is one of the seven deadly sins and thinks cigarette smoke comes straight up from Hell."

"But I am using the veils, am I not, Peter?"

"Veils! They're more like see-through serviettes."

"But I have two big ones, darling."

"That's why the veils won't cover them, Tora. The last one you throw off for the finale wouldn't cover a cream jug."

Tora hung her head modestly, just as though she had clothes on and had been discovered with a button undone. She gazed at me from the tops of her huge eyes. "Perhaps I am a woman who wants to be—how you say in English—emancipated."

"That's impossible, honey. You've run out of veils, so to speak."

"No, Peter, I mean e-*man*-cipated—given to a man in bedlock. I would like to be marry-ed."

"And have a proper white bedding, with me acting as your bed man?"

"You could not be my bed man; you would be my bridesman."

"So who is the lucky fellow you want to marry, dear?"

"Who else but you, Peter, if you are my bridesman to whom I am given in bedlock?"

"Me! But I have already been spoken for, by Olga."

"What is Olga saying?"

"Olga is saying that we'll get married as soon as the business is on its feet or I'll go to church feet first in a coffin."

Tora pouted demurely as she picked up her tiny veils. "Oh, what a shocking waste of so much manpower, Peter. Never mind, I shall still continue to dance for you."

"Please, Tora, please, for my sake, could you dance in the bedroom? You see, these old fuddy-duddies around here are so conventional. They come into the shop and expect you to have clothes on. The Dance of the Seven Veils is an aesthetically perfect art form but they're just not ready for it."

Tora clapped her hands delightedly and laughed her wonderful laugh. "Oh, darling, of course I will dance for you in the bedroom! I was beginning to think you would never ask me. From now on shall I dance for you in the bedroom every night. Then, as the song is saying, I shall dance for you at your wedding."

I closed my eyes in extreme mental distress, certain that either I would eventually wake up from this nightmare or that I had finally succumbed to the dreaded occupational hazard known as the Little Nells. But I did not wake up—and could not go to sleep either—yet Fate's hardest blow was reserved for tomorrow.

There was nothing new about it because William Congreve had tried to warn me earlier—nearly three centuries earlier in fact—when he wrote: 'Heaven has no rage like love to hatred turned, nor hell a fury like a woman scorned'.

It wasn't Olga either.

11

At last I had found a home for the bear. Honners, who could never refuse a gift, decided there was a niche for it at The Hall in the Empire Gallery among the lions, tigers and other game his ancestors had shot in the course of conquering the Empire for Queen Victoria.

"Our family motto has always been this," Honners told me airily. "If it shines buy it; if it's old capture it; if it moves shoot it. That is why we have the largest collection of treasure outside the Tower of London. Unfortunately, when my illustrious forbear, Sir Peregrine Pilkington-Goldberg, tried to add the Tower of London to our collection he received the King's height-reducing treatment by having his head cut off. 'Note well, gentlemen,' said the King, 'how all my enemies are four feet tall.' So Sir Peregrine lost his head in a crisis."

I was visiting Honners at The Hall to deliver the bear, but more importantly to unburden myself to him and seek advice. He listened to my tale of woe with that smug expression on his face of holier-than-thou, although when I came to the harrowing parts he smiled sympathetically and said, "What a mess you're in! Glad it's not me," or "You'll be lucky to get away with five years if she doesn't murder you first."

Eventually I had to say to my friend, "Look, Honners, I'm in desperate trouble and I came to you for advice and consolation."

Honners looked hurt. "Dear comrade of my childhood, advice and consolation you shall have because they cost nothing and are worth less. There are several paths open to you, but let us discount suicide because it is too dangerous, and emigration because you are penniless."

"What are the other paths then, comrade of my childhood? Or are they too horrible to contemplate?"

Honners patted my arm reassuringly. "First the good news, Peter. We must keep you alive at all costs because you owe me a lot of money."

"Oh joy! Why didn't I come to you sooner?"

"And we must keep you out of jail so you can earn it to repay me as soon as possible."

"What is this rare gift you possess of making troubles vanish into thin air?"

"I want you to know, Peter, that for old times' sake I'm not leaning on you for it," Honners said sincerely. "Just keep to the mortgage contract date we signed at my solicitors."

"You are generous to a fault, Honners. How did you manage to stay so rich when you're so magnanimous? Was there so much that you didn't miss the pennies?"

Honners poured himself a scotch and lit a cigar. "So, Peter, we've already disposed of your major headache. What else really matters?"

"But I didn't come to see you about the mortgage, Honners. The knife at my throat is Tora. Then there's the Constable painting hanging over my head."

"Yes, Peter, there it is hanging over your head just behind you. Beautiful, isn't it?"

"But the police still think I nicked it in the first place."

"Suspicious lot. Find the thief and shame them, say I—

always assuming it wasn't you, of course."

"You don't really believe I stole from you, surely, Honners?"

"Never entered my head. But with the picture safe and sound it might pay to confess with tears and get a lighter sentence. You know the drill these days—been drinking, moment of temptation, hid painting for a joke, panicked, afraid of consequences, lesson learned, never do it again, good character, couldn't sleep for twenty years, needed money, over-worked, took to drugs, wife gone off with milkman, lost on the horses, amnesia through war wounds, unemployed, house struck by lightning, living in tent. . . ."

"The judge would reckon I'd be better off in prison, mate. You'd get me ten years' protective custody. You'll find this hard to believe, Honners, but my immediate problem is women,—and I mean Tora because she is more than a woman —she's women."

Honners waved my discomfiture aside. "Your trouble is that you go around like a woman's plaything and become involved."

"Me! Everyone knows I'm emotional steel."

"Slightly wrong, Peter. You're emotional mud. Now, to rip Tora off your back you need brains, so that eliminates you for a start—but is the obvious cue for me. I can disperse Tora completely given time—I shall need all of three minutes."

I laughed mirthlessly. "Not a chance, Honners. She's in and she's determined to stay. You couldn't pull her out with a tractor."

"Then watch the master at work. With my inimitable panache I shall impersonate the Norwegian Ambassador phoning from London. The import of my message will be that

Tora has been honoured by a request to prepare designs for modern statuary to decorate the embassy and is required for preliminary consultation in London forthwith if not sooner."

"You sure do think fast, Honners," I said admiringly.

"Nothing, nothing, little commoner. Only last year we had, among other top CD brass, the Norwegian Ambassador here at The Hall for the Hunt Ball, so I have plenty of authentic chitchat at my fingertips for the purpose. It may smack of chicanery but what would I not do for a friend in need? Am I the person who would desert a pal in his hour of distress? Is it in my generous nature to withhold the hand of succour to a comrade in trouble?"

"Of course not, Honners, because in the past you've always let me down left, right and centre."

"Even I cannot succeed in all I undertake. Incidentally, I shall have to ask you for expenses. The phone call's a pound, plus a fiver service charge."

"Six sheets!"

"What a bargain to be free of Tora before Olga flies in, camel-sore, sand eroded, sunburned and oil-polluted. Think on that and go around shouting 'Honners is king! Double his fee!'"

Having paid Honners six pounds, I left The Hall in an easier state of mind. He had promised to phone at six, half an hour before Tora took her evening shower, guaranteeing to remove the lady from the premises by an early train the next day. After that it was my task to keep her out once the subterfuge was discovered by closing the shop for the short time till Olga's return, hiding myself as though the business was unoccupied and I had flown.

The call rang at six precisely. I answered the phone and

listened spellbound to Honners in character; the formal language of diplomacy, the subtle foreign accent, the authentic background details. All he lacked was snow-skis. It was such an impressive performance that I automatically addressed him as Excellency, as I had heard on the movies.

I handed the phone to Tora with a courtly bow. "His Excellency the Norwegian Ambassador would give you audience."

"The Norwegian Ambassador!" Tora gasped. "For me!"

"There's only two of us here, darling, and he doesn't want me."

"But why is he phoning me, Peter?"

"The best way to find out is to ask him."

"Oh, I am so frightened, so nervous."

"How you've changed, Tora."

"I have seen his picture and he is such a lovely handsome man. So big and strong, so attractive to women. He is like a god."

"Let's hope he's a patient god or he'll ring off."

"There must be some mistake, Peter," Tora said, automatically arranging her hair. "How can I dare to answer our Ambassador when I am not properly dressed?"

"He won't know you're in the nude, dear."

"I was about to take a bath, Peter. I feel dreadful."

"Pop upstairs and slap a tiara on your head."

"But I should be dressed formally."

"Long gloves and tights too?"

"You know very well what I mean, Peter. The traditional dress when one is invited to Court."

"No tie and handcuffs?"

"Not the police court. St. James's."

166

"Well, you certainly haven't got time to dress now, Tora."

So saying, I made a quick voice check to see if Honners was still at the other end, then thrust Tora on the phone quite unceremoniously.

Hearing a two-way dialogue strike up I glided off to the workshop with an immeasurable sense of relief that Honners had found a method of prising Tora out of my life before Olga returned. In the workshop I passed the time beeswaxing a Sheraton satinwood Pembroke table, crossbanded in king-wood and inlaid with ebony. Such was my loss of tension that I hummed and sang a traditional trade polishing shanty as I worked:

Burnish copper, polish wood; Rub away and make them nice.

Shiny brassware looks so good; This is how we raise the price.

Beeswaxing was particularly restful to my present state of mind, being a simple process, soothing and safe. After all, one could hardly have a serious accident with beeswax, and Olga had forbade my using the electric sander since my experience with a long toasting fork. This had unfortunately become caught up in the drive-spindle to the extent that it had wrapped itself around the shaft in the spiral shape of a clock spring.

Suddenly my attention was attracted by a kind of female mating call from behind. Turning round at my bench I was alarmed to see the moon face of Sonia at the rear window.

"It's me—Sonia," she informed me, as though I was working by night.

I ran to the window to block her out lest Tora returned from the phone. "Sorry, dear, but we're closed," I said lamely.

"*We?*" Sonia asked archly.

"The shop, dear. It's gone six."

"I'm not a customer, darling. I'm your lover—remember? Why haven't you been to see me for so long?"

"Too busy, dear. I'm sorry but I've been under pressure handling one or two difficult clients. I'll be round at the first possible opportunity, sweetheart."

Sonia smiled. "I understand, darling. My dad told me how Olga had gone off and left you to manage alone. What a shame!"

"I've been struggling on the best I can, Sonia," I replied modestly. "The show must go on, you know. That's life. Tough, but it's only for a month."

"Poor Peter! If only you'd told me I would have been round to help you. I've done shop work before and I loved it."

"Thanks a million, Sonia, but I've managed somehow. I just shut the shop when I had to go out buying or delivering."

"My dad told me you had a woman in to look out for you."

I swallowed hard. Just how much had Constable Barrington told his daughter? Even worse, just how much had Sonia told him? I felt the nutcrackers round me.

"Yes, dear, there was a lady living nearby who kindly popped in when I was really stuck."

"My dad told me she was staying here with you, Peter."

I laughed merrily. "Ah, I expect he guessed that, dear. Saw her once or twice and assumed she was living here."

"My dad told me how you said she was living here because she was Olga's stepsister."

"Well, I suppose so, really, to be exact about it, you know how it is. . . ."

168

"My dad told me she's foreign and very dishy."

"Some folks might say that. Actually, she's an extremely quiet, homely sort of girl. Spends most of her time reading and knitting."

"My dad told me she spends most of her time belly-dancing with precious little on."

"Only because she's keen on keep fit. She regards dancing as a kind of exercise, like Swedish drill."

"My dad told me she isn't half sexy and she's got a figure like she was pumped up."

"Don't mind my saying this, Sonia, but your dad seems to have told you an awful lot, as if he's got an almost morbid interest in Tora."

"My dad thinks it's you who's got a morbid interest in Tora. My dad tells me pretty well everything, Peter."

"I hope you don't tell him everything, dear. About us, I mean."

"Oh, Peter, just because my dad's a policeman doesn't mean I blab everything to him. Besides, I never gossip about people who keep their word. Of course, I might grass on someone who broke his word."

I was sweating already. Sonia was putting on the pressure and Tora might appear at any moment with hot Corps Diplomatique news about rushing off to cement up the Norwegian embassy. I swore on oath that, once clear of the present entanglements, I would forsake the female gender completely. I wondered if monks in their cloistered cells were actually antique dealers whose involvement with women had driven them to renounce the lusts of the flesh behind the safety of stone walls built on remote islands. Suddenly I had a flash of inspiration born of despair.

"Olga's stepsister leaves tomorrow, dear, so then we can be together again just like old times—that is assuming your husband is still abroad."

"Dont you worry your head about Jim. His firm told me his bus broke down in some jungle—India I think, or was it Malaysia?—so they're flying new parts out to him. Anyhow, it means he won't be home for Christmas like he promised. The way he's going on he could settle out there and raise a family for all I'd know about it."

But I was worrying about Jim because his prolonged absence meant no relief for me in that quarter. My sole remaining hope was that the real thief of the Constable painting would be apprehended, so I would not be dependent on Sonia's alibi.

Sonia inserted a large hand through the window and placed it possessively on my arm. "Now Olga's stepsister is leaving I'll be round tomorrow, love. In time to cook lunch for you too."

I smiled falsely, as if my facial muscles had suddenly shrunk and stretched my lips. "That would be wonderful, Sonia, but I thought how nice it would be if I came round to your place now Jim is definitely stuck overseas."

"Whatever for? I want to help you run the business, look after you and . . . well, you know . . . make sure you're not lonely at night sort of."

I glanced round apprehensively for signs of Tora but her voice was still discernible from within. Nevertheless, I estimated time must be running out.

"To be frank with you, Sonia," I pleaded, dropping my features into confidential pose that women like and whispering from the back of my hand into a big red ear, "what with trying to run the shop without Olga, having the picture theft on my plate, and *her* bossing me about . . . you know what I mean."

I emphasized such a very long *her* by inclining my eyeballs to the right as I had seen Olga do, that Sonia nodded in tacit understanding of how trying other women could be. I was not slow to perceive her reaction.

"Well, dear, what with *her* telling me how to run my own business and me trying to keep the peace, and, worst of all . . . but I won't go into details now while she's still on the premises but I expect you can guess."

Sonia nodded sympathetically at my plight. "So you see, dear, that I'm completely worn out. What I want more than anything right now is to shut the shop till Olga returns and come round to you for a complete rest. Recharge the batteries and try to forget what I've been through. Nobody could do that better for me than you—darling."

Sonia gripped my arm like a vice to assure me she understood, and that it took a woman like her to repair the damage wrought by a woman like Tora. "I'll take care of you and drive all your troubles away, Peter," she confirmed archly. "See you in time for lunch tomorrow then. I'll start you off with a nice big man-meal—rump steak and beer, eh? Give us a kiss on account."

I foolishly leaned over the window-still for a farewell peck and found myself almost dragged into the yard. "Plenty more where that came from, Peter," she threatened me on release. "See you tomorrow—naughty boy!"

Directly Sonia disappeared I returned to vigorous beeswaxing in order to reduce trembling and to regroup my mind. None too soon either, because Tora glided in wearing the familiar economy rig of towel-turban and sandals—strapless, of course.

"Hello, darling; did I hear you talking to someone while I was upon the phone?" she asked, kissing my sweaty forehead.

Why, I wondered, were women endowed with such strong curiosity, forcing me to live in a world of lies? "No, Tora. I was merely singing at my work. Always sing when I'm happy —like right now."

"Strange. Perhaps it was a two-part song and you were taking both baritone and soprano, yes?"

"Any luck with the Norwegian Ambassador, darling?"

"What do you mean, any luck? How can one be lucky with one's Ambassador?"

"I mean was it good news; anything important you might want to tell me about?"

"How can one have good news from one's Ambassador, Peter? I am not understanding."

"Well . . . surely one's Ambassador doesn't ring one every day of the week, so I thought perhaps one had heard something special that one would like to share with another one."

Tora smiled smugly. "The Ambassador is asking me to design some modern sculpture to capture the spirit of Norwegians abroad and particularly in this country."

"Marvellous! What an honour! You could sculpt a Viking in a vintage car entitled 'The Model T Fjord'."

Tora groaned. " 'The Model T Fjord'—oh, Peter, how could you!"

Lately I had become rather worried at the way people groaned when I made a witticism, so I was cutting down on them. "No doubt you'll want to leave for London at the first possible opportunity," I said sadly.

"Why should I do that, Peter?"

"Well, I suppose the Ambassador will wish to discuss plans with you. I bet you can't wait to get started. The train I usually catch leaves Cudford at 8.20. Of course, you may prefer to avoid the rush on the 7.20. Actually, the first one is the 6.20—bags of room for feet up."

Tora pulled off the towel-turban and shook free her long fair tresses. "Sounds as though you want to be rid of me, Peter," she pouted. "A lot of men would be delighted to have me here."

"That's the lot of men who aren't expecting Olga back, dear."

"But I've promised to go before she returns, darling. Now you seem to want me to leave earlier."

"Oh, Tora, nobody wishes you to stay more than I do. Since you arrived it's been the happiest ten years off my life."

"Then I have good news for you, darling—I'm not going."

Shock can surprise even an actor of my calibre, to the extent that my jaw dropped and eyes widened before I could register unbounded joy. "Splendid news, dear. How come I am so lucky? Won't your Ambassador be upset?"

"My Ambassador is upset already because I am telling him he is not my Ambassador but someone making joke in—how you say?—making joke in very bad smell. Then he is losing his temper and screaming and swearing at me. I am the victim of a hox. Some nasty man is making me hox-ed."

My heart sank as Sonia's picture rose in my mind like the sun coming up. "What on earth makes you think it was a hoax, Tora?"

"Because I am discovering that this Norwegian Ambassador

will not speak Norwegian, and when I am asking him why he says it is the new rule issued by our Government that he must speak only English while he is in this country. So I am setting a little trap for him. I am saying in Norwegian how I have learned that a bomb is timed to explode in his office in one hour, then this imposter is asking me to repeat it in English because I am breaking the new rule agreed upon at the United Nations. So I say in English that I have lost my passport, and this hox man tells me he will issue a new one when we meet in London. He must be a larger fool than he thinks I am."

"Certainly sounds like some pactical joker is at work, dear. I should forget it."

I wanted to forget it too. Honners possessed a rare gift of mimicry which never quite came off, partly through over-confidence and partly through his inability to control his temper. Useless imitating the Archbishop of Canterbury if you scream abuse the moment you can't have your own way.

Tora began playing idly with my broken nose. "Peter darling," she purred, "do you know anyone round here who keeps a parrot or mynah bird?"

"I hope the feel of my nose hasn't prompted that remark, dear. As a matter of fact I do. Honners keeps a parrot up at The Hall. Reckons it's better than any guard-dog."

"Does it talk?"

"Never stops. That's because it's Honners'. Why do you ask?"

"Well, when I was on the phone just now a voice in the background kept screaming, 'Call me Master, you seed-snaffling feather-duster! Call me Master, you seed-snaffling feather-duster!' Quite a coincidence, I am sure."

I cursed Honners and all his works, swearing to myself

that never again would I accept his help and all the trouble it led to, like throwing a lifebelt to a drowning man cunningly fashioned in lead.

That night I went to bed in chastened mood, thinking how my affairs were at their lowest ebb, so any development must be for the better. But just how wrong can a man be?

12

Tora was a real classy doll who did everything to perfection—
and that's how she slept. How she could sleep! She didn't so
much drop off as lie down and die. Sometimes I wondered if
the long Arctic winter of her country caused men to kiss their
wives goodnight and say, "Switch off the light, dear, and
sleep well. See you in the Spring."

When first she came to ruin my life I carried up two cups
of coffee as a nightcap, only to discover she had passed away.
I shook her, bellowed in her ear—even sat her up in bed—to
no avail. Worried, I leaned over her and listened for any sound
of breathing. Eventually I detected a slight up-and-down movement at the only place she could not hide it, her bosom. So,
ever the gentleman, I gently grasped her ankles and slid her
down flat again, then drank both coffees.

When Tora lay on her back she often emitted a soft, regular
snore that I switched off by rolling her onto her side. I soon
discovered that one did not have to be too gentle about this
because one night I accidentally pushed her so hard that she
rolled over too far and fell out of bed onto the carpet. I lifted
her back to the mattress feeling extremely brutal but she
did not wake at all.

Personally, I am an in-between sleeper—not light, not
heavy—but the current worries had turned me into such an
insomniac that, once I had managed to drop off into a quick

nightmare, the slightest noise would rouse me. Like a tap dripping downstairs in the kitchen, or the ticking of Tora's wristwatch. Frankly I had come to dread the long nights, during which I either suffered hideous dreams or lay awake trying to recover from them. Thus for the first time in my life I was forced to resort to some of Olga's sleeping-pills. Now I quickly went to sleep, only to endure nightmares I couldn't wake up from. So I gave those up too, preferring short horror films to continuous performances.

One awful night I awoke to find myself naked in the bath, trying to scrub my body with a brush and no water. I read in a psychology book that this indicated my efforts to wash away the results of a guilty conscience, so henceforth I locked the kitchen door at night in case I tried out the gas-oven.

Thursday night I lay trembling in bed, recovering from a short visit to Tyburn and wondering how badly my neck had been broken after I had been lynched by a howling mob of antique dealers led by Bernie Edelstein. Judge Mellon had sentenced me for robbing the Tower of London and making off with the crown jewels, which Bow Street Runner Barrington had espied on sale in my shop window. The first time I was hanged from the gibbet a message arrived from the King granting me a pardon, so they cut me down. But I was strung up again for the Constable painting, only to be cut down once more because the real thief had been apprehended. I lay there feeling like a yo-yo when a warrant arrived from Olga, whereupon I was hanged a third time.

In the darkness I sprawled on the bed, convinced my neck was three feet long and wondering if the gibbet would have to be raised to accommodate my new length for the next hanging.

It was then I heard the burglar. In my dazed condition I thought at first it was a messenger bringing yet another warrant for my execution, but gradually I realized we had a visitor on the premises. I turned to Tora and it crossed my mind that if I attacked the intruder using her as a club she still wouldn't wake. I grabbed my anti-bandit cosh from the bedside-table to give me confidence but the cosh wouldn't stop shaking, just as if it was alive. Someone was creeping up the stairs so carefully that there were no footsteps but a considerable amount of creaking. This indicated a big thug.

I am by nature a bold courageous fellow, fearless to a fault, caring little for any man and completely immune to ghosts or other spirit manifestations. The type you can depend on in a pub fracas or leave alone in a haunted castle for the night. In fact I had often reassured Olga that if a burglar ever dared show his face in our house it would be his last job because I should be compelled to take him apart before handing him over to the police in a bucket.

Consequently I was not a little surprised to find myself unable to move to the point of paralysis, lying there motionless on a bed which insisted upon shaking so much that it communicated itself to the cosh. My cosh was not only vibrating but hitting me in the process. I knew I must protect Sleeping Beauty next to me, so I hoped she would wake up sufficiently to appreciate my gallantry as I died for her. My mind did a quick check on our insurance policy payments in case I was overpowered and lost our stock-in-trade. Fortunately Olga had ensured we were fully paid up, leading me to speculate whether it would not be wiser to feign slumber and let the burglar take all he could carry.

But cowardice is entirely foreign to my nature so I determined to fight it out if only I could jump out of bed for the affray. I discovered by experiment that I could not get out of bed even very slowly, nor could I sit up. I decided to attack the intruder lying down, thinking how this novel stratagem might well confuse him and leave him a helpless victim to my vibrating cosh. Further to increase my advantage I pulled the quilt over my head, shut my eyes and concentrated upon reducing my shake-rate. I could only conclude that my body was consuming so much energy in trembling that there was none left for other movement, but I felt confident that when the critical moment arrived I should once more be the fearless snarling tiger of yore.

Without warning a voice whispered, "Is that you, Peter?"

I squealed with shock, for here was a burglar who knew my name. "No." I said cunningly. "This is Butch, and there are six more guys from the heavy mob in the other rooms."

"But I've checked the other rooms and they're empty."

"We saw you break in, so they're hiding in ambush. One shout from me and you're a dead duck."

I had to repeat this three times because my tongue kept rolling up like a spring and parking in my pharynx.

"Go on—shout if you dare!"

I tried to shout but nothing more than a hiss emerged. My mouth was as dry as if it was full of sulphur, so that I could not disengage my teeth from my lips and cheeks. It seemed that my entire shouting equipment had seized up in a fleshy goo. Then an extraordinary thing happened. The burglar drew back the quilt and started to get into bed beside me. So it wasn't robbery after all, I gasped to myself, but premeditated rape such as one reads about in the popular press. I decided to sell myself dearly, though I had reservations about the Victorian maxim recommending death before dishonour.

"Shove up a bit and give me some room," the voice said.

"Who are you? I'm not in the habit of sharing with strangers."

"Come off it, Peter. It's me, of course."

"I know a great many me's. Which me are you?"

"Put your hand here and guess, Peter."

I shrieked into the night. It was a female. A large female. "Sonia!" I cried. "I can feel your nearness."

"Peter love! We're together at last. I guessed something awful must have happened when you didn't turn up so I hurried to your side. I just couldn't wait. You know what a state I get in without my man. Now we're alone together with the whole night before us."

"How on earth did you manage to come in, Sonia."

"Simple. Through your workshop window. It wasn't fastened. I guessed you did that deliberately—for me. How romantic of you, just like Romeo and Juliet."

"Of course, dear," I groaned, cursing my carelessness and perplexed as to how Romeo and Juliet came into it.

Already Sonia was trembling with assorted neuroses, as I divined from her eight hands. "Goodness gracious, you lovely manny man—what . . . ever . . . is . . . this . . . down . . . here!" she demanded archly.

"That's my anti-bandit cosh, Sonia."

"Oh! How brave of you, darling. You thought I might be a burglar, yet you were prepared to fight him off without a thought for your own safety. I adore strong men like you but I shudder to think how you might have coshed me in the dark.

"Naturally I was ready for any eventuality, Sonia," I admitted modestly, thinking that she might still have to be coshed if Tora woke up. My left hand lay lightly on Tora even now lest she turned onto her back for the Sleeping Sentry lullaby.

"When did Olga's stepsister go off, Peter?"

"About two hours ago," I said truthfully.

"Oo, how late. You said you'd get shot of her before lunch. So that's why you couldn't come round to me, you poor boy. Anyway, we can make up for lost time now. Just give me another inch for your big girl."

I gave Sonia exactly an inch and no more because, although the bed was the Continental five-footer, I had my left arm hooked round Tora lest she fell out the other side. I lay between the two women bewildered and scared lest each should discover the other, especially now that Sonia was preparing to crush me in the rites of love. I figured that if I did my duty for England she might be persuaded to go home, though for the life of me I couldn't think of a valid reason in which the cosh did not loom large. The other problem was that I had become utterly unsexed with fear, which had left me about as lustful as a fried egg, but just as I was wondering how Sonia would make love to her male corpse there came the most urgent rat-tat-tat at the front door such as is employed only by the landlord when you are pretending to be out on rent day. It echoed through the house, then was immediately repeated, as though the caller imagined I slept behind the door and could open it without getting up.

"Somebody at the front door, Peter," Sonia informed me in case desire had sent me deaf. "Who can that be at one in the morning? The way you are tonight, no wonder they call it the small hours."

"Let it be and they'll go away," I replied, unable to face anybody under the circumstances.

But the knocking continued so loudly and insistently that I dreaded it would wake Tora. "Better pop down and see what it is, loverboy," Sonia advised me.

I tried not to panic at the thought of leaving Sonia in the same bed with Tora. "Darling, I'm a bit shaken up after the scare tonight. Would you come down with me, please?"

"But I'm only a helpless female, Peter."

"I know, love, but there's a lot of you . . . I mean, at least it's reassuring to have company."

Sonia squeezed my hand like a mangle. "Two heads are better than one, eh darling?"

"Yes, especially if it's somebody carrying a cosh."

After lending Sonia an old dressing-gown I led her downstairs to the telephone, thankful to have got her clear of the bedroom but perturbed by the hammering from without.

"You answer the door, Sonia, while I stay here to ring the police if it's a nasty customer outside. The door is on the chain," I whispered.

"No thanks, Peter. The chain's not much good if he's armed with a gun."

Sonia was adamant that ringing the police wasn't more dangerous than opening the door, so I crept forward on tiptoe to call through the letter-box, "Who's there?"

"Gawd love us, Pook, you come at last!" boomed a familiar voice. "I was just about to bust your door down."

"Constable Barrington!" I cried, partly from shock, partly to warn Sonia to hide.

"Suppose you thought it was Father Christmas. Open up in the name of the lawwer."

My nerves made me disengage the chain as if I was knitting it, and sweat poured off me. Once the door was open I blocked the aperture with my body less he rushed through and seized his daughter. Constable Barrington shone his torch right in my face, isolated his large eyeballs and exclaimed, "Lumme, a corpus delicti!"

"Guilty, m'lud," I moaned hopelessly.

"Oh, so you done it deliberate, eh?"

"No, it just happened."

"Then why don't you lock the damned thing?"

"What thing, Constable?"

"The window I found open in the course of me night check. You'd be the first to complain if your shop got done over, yet you leaves the workshop window wide open. Might as well leave the front door open as well."

"Is that all you came for?" I gasped incredulously.

"Ain't that enough? What else do you expect—the police band and motor-cycle display team?"

"I can't thank you enough for what you've done tonight, Constable. I'll fasten the window and ensure it never happens again. How fortunate we are to have such a vigilant detective force in Cudford."

"Do you want me to check that no villain climbed in?"

"You're busy enough, Constable. I'll do that right away. All's well, as they used to say in the days of the old Night Watch. Good-night, sir."

When Constable Barrington had departed Sonia appeared and was actually giggling. "Good thing my dad didn't know I'm here," she chuckled. "He'd have killed you."

"Please don't giggle, dear. Just go home. I'm beat."

"Poor Peter. This is when you need me most. Let me help

you back to bed, then I'll make you forget all your worries."

My legs were so frail that I leaned on Sonia's arms while she assisted me to climb the stairs, finally sprawling on the bed so weakened that there seemed little I could do to protect my defenceless body from her demands.

Once Sonia had parked me horizontally to her satisfaction she whispered in my ear, "Before we soar to the moon together, darling, I thought you would like to know that my dad has found out everything."

"He knows you're here with me?" I gasped, wondering if balloons can soar.

"Heaven forbid! He would kill you. I mean about the Constable painting. He knows you're innocent."

"A fine time to tell me that, Sonia!"

"The picture was stolen by Mrs Kendal's husband, Billy Kendal. He died soon afterwards, so she was stuck with it all those years until she sold it to you, Peter."

"Why didn't Constable Barrington tell me before?"

"Because you courted me long ago. He wanted you to suffer for that as long as possible."

"So now I've got to suffer some more, Sonia."

"No, darling, because I'm going to love all your troubles away as only a woman like me can. In fact you will soon begin to imagine there must be two women in your bed."

When Cudford Townhall clock struck four I felt I had been awake for the best part of a week. Sonia dozed contentedly by my side, so I did not move lest I woke her. To this end I lay as one dead, staring at the ceiling to concoct a plan to get her out of the house before daybreak. Time was running out, for directly the sun rose on my harem there would be no hiding the girls from each other, and you couldn't hide Sonia from

184

anyone. I had aged considerably during the night, certain I was a little old man of eighty who had accidentally fallen into bad company.

While I lay rigid as a frozen duck in a supermarket an arm embraced me which was far too slim for Sonia's. I did a quick identity check and discovered it was Tora's. "Hello, Superman," she growled.

I winced because when Tora growled it meant she had awakened fit and refreshed from slumber and sought her jungle mate for aggressive love. Already I could feel her bosom heaving like the incoming tide and her supple body hot with passion. I reflected that I seemed to be the central figure in group therapy.

"Hello, darling," I grunted wearily.

"Why are you whispering, Peter?"

"Think I've lost my voice. Could you keep yours down too, please dear?"

"Whatever for?"

"So we don't disturb the neighbours. You know how they complain."

"I only said hello, Peter—we're not holding an all-night party."

"Just play it cool, dear, there's a good girl. I've got a bit of a headache."

"The best cure for a headache is violent love, darling. It circulates the blood and relieves tension. You must leap about the bed screaming your mating-call while I fight you off. But because you are big strong man I soon have to surrender, and then you rubbish me."

"Ugh!" The exclamation slipped out before I could halt it.

"Oh, so now it is ugh! You no longer want me, eh?"

"I think I am sick, Tora."

"Sick of me is it, you Peter you?"

"No, darling. I'm not well."

"So what is making you not well? Is it another woman?"

"What on earth would I want with another woman, dear?" I whispered, automatically expanding my chest to conceal Sonia.

"There is something strange about you, tonight, Peter. You are a bundle of nerves, you whisper, you do not move, you keep me on the edge of the bed, you do not attack me, and you smell of cheap perfume. It is this cheap perfume that is waking me up, not your mad passionate stupor."

"My new aftershave, honey."

"Aftershave! Huh! Then they are selling you big poof perfume instead. Tell me you love me, Peter."

"I love you, dear."

"Don't exhaust yourself with ardent words, but on the other hand you don't need to grunt it like a motto. Let me hear those magic words again from your lifeless lips."

"I love you, dear."

"I love you too, darling—you're so romantic with me."

"Who said that!" Tora exclaimed sharply.

"I did dear. Merely mimicking your reply in fun, like this." My voice shot up to falsetto, reciting *Mary had a little Lamb*, partly because my nerves had snapped, partly to drown any further dialogue from Sonia.

"Who said 'Who said that?' "

"Who's that saying 'Who said who said that?' "

"Good heavens, who's that in the bed!"

"Is that another woman in the bed!"

186

"Who the devil are you!"

"What are you doing here!"

"Quick, Peter, switch the light on. There's a female in the bed!"

I lay petrified as the storm raged over me, unable to move, let alone find the light switch over by the door. Yet in some unaccountable way the light came on of its own accord, revealing Olga standing by it. Her mouth was so wide open that I feared lockjaw. Mine was even wider. Tora and Sonia both looked as though they were at the dentists. We were all frozen in tonsil inspection pose for several seconds before anybody was capable of speech.

Olga was first to break the silence with a shattering triple oath one hears only when a dealer drops a Georgian spatter glass epergne while dressing a high display shelf. I had no idea Olga knew such language, "I arrive home a day early and what do I find?" she fumed.

I kept silent because we all knew what she had found.

"I find Pook in bed with his harem!"

"I can explain. . . ."

"Don't you dare tell me it's the accommodation shortage in Cudford, you conniving little sultan you. Two busty broads in one bed! Two!"

"It's not my fault it's two, dear. . . ."

"Shut up if you're going to tell me it should only have been one, as if that would have been quite in order."

"Of course not. . . ."

"Nor will I believe you're ill and need two nude night nurses."

"I can exp. . . ."

"And don't tell me you've turned Mohammedan and need

187

one more wife for a set."

"I can. . . ."

"Or you missed me so much you wanted somebody to talk to during the long hours of the night. Two bodies in fact."

"I. . . ."

"Try singing it if you stutter. That helps, even when you're lying."

"I can explain everything, Olga. I can explain everything —to all four of us."

Everyone went silent in fascinated expectation of my story. Me included.